A QUESTION OF SANCTUARY

P A WILSON

FREE EBOOK

Claim your copy of A Choice to Make when you sign up for my newsletter and get a glimpse of Lena and Brian at the end of the plagues.

Ebook ISBN: 978-1-927669-88-4
Paperback ISBN: 978-1-927669-89-1
Audio book ISBN:978-1-927669-90-7

CHAPTER ONE

The farmhouse kitchen was warm and fragrant from the morning's baking. Lena shelled peas with Scott beside her, his presence making her feel safe and grounded. The vegetables would be preserved for the winter. She watched as Mellow and Tik cleaned the dishes. This was her dream all that time ago when she walked out of the city. This peaceful scene.

It had been six months. Scott was still not completely back to normal and without antibiotics, it would be a long time before he was, but Lena no longer worried infections would take him. Now his weakness and determination to ignore it was causing concern. Too much too soon would set him back.

Brian had not yet succeeded in finding a place within the community. Lena didn't see any value coming from him. He wandered off when work was needed and claimed to be thinking about the future when she asked him. He wasn't satisfied and took very few pains to hide the feeling. Lena suspected the others were as tired of his constant nit picking as she was.

But it had also been six months without anyone attacking.

The alliance hadn't been tested beyond a bit of skill transferring; the promise of help in an emergency still just that, and it could stay that way forever. She wondered if this was the new reality. If it was, she'd consider every hardship they'd endured to get here worthwhile.

The only blip in the peace was the current encampment of city refugees. The unwelcome visitors would be leaving soon no matter what they planned. The farm was too small to support so many unskilled people. Perhaps Brian would leave with them. His talents proved more useful in larger groups.

"I heard a rumor from the camp," Scott said.

"You've been hanging out with them? Be careful; I'm not sure they know how to keep their camp clean enough. We can't be sure there's no illness lurking." Lena wanted to keep Scott isolated so he wouldn't contract yet another infection. Her logical mind knew it was useless, but death was too easy now. And she didn't know how she'd continue without Scott. The only thing she knew for certain was that she wouldn't return to Brian. Her marriage was dead and buried long ago.

"They're fine." He took the colander of peas to the sink. "A few more come every day. We can't let them camp much longer. Unless you think we can use the labor in the fields?"

"I'm more worried they'll harvest the crops and leave us with nothing," Lena said. "What rumor?"

"A preacher. He's telling everyone we need to repent so God will not send another plague."

"And people believe him?" She wasn't entirely surprised. The plagues happened because people believed nonsense about vaccinations and stopped getting their kids vaccinated. It got so bad, herd immunity was gone and enough people died that civilization collapsed.

"There are a lot of people who don't have what we do," Scott said. "They are scared, and he's charismatic. People will believe anything if someone is promising safety."

"Should we keep the refugees around so we can field an army?" Lena laughed, but Scott looked serious. "Maybe we should reach out to our allies? Find out what they know?"

Tik looked at Lena from where he was drying dishes. "Isn't that a bit alarmist? There's no problem here. Well, apart from the camp."

He has a point.

"Better too early than too late," she said. "But let's deal with the refugees first. I need to find Brian. He knows how to talk to them."

Mellow wiped her hands and cocked her head toward the back door. "He went out an hour ago. He does that a lot, goes for a walk when there's work to do."

"Maybe we can persuade him to go for a walk with the refugees," Lena said. "It's more his thing anyway. They are looking for a place to start another town, a big one. He'll have a role in managing the whole enterprise."

"Are you trying out your argument on us?" Tik asked. "We would support you telling him to go even without a plan."

"If I thought that would work, I'd do it," Lena said. "Leaving him in the city when we escaped wasn't enough of a hint our marriage was over. He's ignoring anything that doesn't fit in his worldview, including anything that separates us."

"Well, anything except our bedroom door," Scott said.

"I wouldn't count on that lasting," Mellow said. "I see him pacing the hall at night. Like he's building the courage to burst in and demand his marriage bed."

Lena stifled her laugh. It wasn't fair to do this behind Brian's back. She'd find the time to tell him again there is no future for them as a couple. *Maybe he'll listen this time.* "Let's hope he gets over it," she said. "Is everyone out in the fields?"

"The kids are cleaning out the cellar," Scott said. "We'll need more room for food storage this year even with the share going to the alliance. Keith is hunting. Deb is in the camp offering nursing. She said no illness, but there are lots of minor injuries. And there are a few people who exist in a daze. They need counseling, and she's not the right person for that."

"I wonder what skills they brought. Even if they find a town to inhabit, they'll need workers and teachers and doctors," Mellow said.

"It sounds like they're healthy enough to head out. How they build their future isn't our problem." Lena stood and dumped the pea pods into the stock pot.

CHAPTER TWO

She saw Brian heading toward the house. Telling him to leave always seemed easy, but when an opportunity came up, she never found the right words. The problem was practical; Brian didn't fit in and wasn't even trying. He had to go. The solution felt a bit too harsh when she tried to simply say the words. No one wanted to send someone out on the road these days. This time she was saved by someone knocking at the door. *Coward.*

"Are you going to help us or not?" A man stood on the porch, arms crossed.

Lena thought she recognized him from New Surrey, but the camp was made up of five or six towns' worth of people. He could be a stranger. It made no difference. No one from the camp listened to her when she tried to explain her side of the problem. They only talked about their needs.

"Good morning, my name is Lena Custordin. It's my land you're camped on."

He unfolded his arms. "Aron Simons."

He gave her no reason to be polite. "Why should I help

you? I didn't invite you. I didn't agree you could camp here. As far as I'm concerned, you should go on your way."

He took a step forward as if to enter the house. Lena squared her shoulders and stayed firmly planted in front of the door.

"Your husband told us we could stay," he said.

"You mean Brian. He is not my husband and has no authority. What do you expect me to do with you?"

The question was genuine. Lena had no idea what made the group of refugees think she had any responsibility for their future. They were lucky that she didn't pick up a gun to get them to move.

"You got here and survived. You've been here long enough to know what's going on in the world. We can't simply keep wandering."

It was the first time anyone from the camp had even answered her question.

"What did you do before you left your city?" If she had any doubts left about fleeing that life, Aron's attitude burned them away. In this new world, people needed to be able to look after themselves first. Alliances and assistance came second.

"I was the comptroller. It means I managed the budget."

"I know what a comptroller did." It must be difficult for him now that no one needed his skills. He'd been important in the old world.

"Fine." He took a half step closer and leaned in to intimidate her. "We've been here a week. When are you going to get off your ass and help us out?"

Entitled bastards didn't last long these days. "Go back to the camp and be very happy I'm not the sort to shoot people who annoy me. Pack up and find a place where you are welcome."

"You won't help?" He seemed genuinely shocked.

"I don't know what I can do to help. Go back to the camp and let me talk to my family."

"There are more of us," Aron said.

So, they were down to threats. "Sure. But how many people have you killed to save your property?"

He got the hint. Lena watched him walk back to the camp. They were leaving in the next few days whether or not she could think of a way that didn't require force. And she didn't think it was a good idea to test the alliance by sending them to Crystal. No one needed a pack of people in their community who wouldn't take responsibility for themselves.

Lena returned to the kitchen. No Brian. A good thing because when she saw him, he would find out how happy she was that he'd invited the refugees. And suddenly she didn't feel so bad about telling him he should join the people in the camp.

Scott and Tik leaned together, talking over a map spread out on the table.

"We heard," Scott said looking up at Lena. "You know they aren't going to give up, right?"

"Unreasonable people can be quite stubborn. And I'm not prepared to shoot anyone to make my point. What can we do to help?"

Tik smoothed the map. "It doesn't need to be only helping them." He looked at Scott. "We have an idea."

Why do I feel like this is going to be a hard one to hear?

"Okay," Lena said. She joined them over the map.

"They don't want to start our kind of community," Scott said. "I'm told they think they can get a city working again if they start from scratch."

"You think there's an empty city nearby?" They hadn't explored much, but Crystal and Redstone were barely more than villages. Prosperity was still more like a commune than a town. "And do you agree with them?"

Scott shook his head. "It doesn't matter if we agree they can reboot a city. Just that they believe they can."

"Why don't they just go back to one of the places they deserted?" As much as she wanted this solution, Lena figured it was only postponing the next demand for help.

"They think the future is west of us. They might be right. The weather gets less extreme the farther west you go. Our idea will help us too, the whole alliance." Scott pointed to the map. "We pick a place and take them there. Far enough away they won't keep visiting for more assistance and their screw ups won't bounce back on any of us."

Lena looked at the map. A few towns sat not that far from the farm. Maybe three weeks to a month's travel. The big cities were too far, but maybe the refugees would settle for a season. "Who takes them?"

Scott looked at Tik, who looked back down at the map.

"Fine," Scott said. "Me and Tik. You can spare us. We need to do some exploring. I can manage that. I don't have the stamina to help with the farm right now. The camp can't travel fast or far in one go. It will give me a chance to build my endurance."

"We can teach them how to survive as we travel," Tik said. "We can both hunt well enough."

"It's a plan," Lena said. "You'll be gone for months, maybe need to winter somewhere. What does Mellow think about the idea?"

"She'll be fine. And the trip won't be that long if we don't go too far west. Three months out and we can come back faster. We can survive a week or so of winter travel."

"You don't need us here," Scott reminded her.

He didn't say she had Brian, but Lena heard the words clearly. "I will always need you. Both of you."

"Not for work," Scott said. "Brian will have to step up if we aren't here."

She could manage without Brian too, if he went. The harvest was in. Keith could hunt for enough food, maybe train Mahir. "I need to know what the city refugees think about it."

"But we need to explore," Tik said. "If they won't go, we should still do that."

Lena held up her hand. "I know, but if they won't agree, I need you here to help get rid of them before we're stuck with them forever."

CHAPTER THREE

Brian finally showed up an hour after Lena saw him approaching the house. He grabbed a tea and one of Mellow's muffins and sat at the table.

"Where have you been?" Lena asked, trying to sound interested rather than pissed off.

"Scouting the area. It's important to keep an eye on what's coming toward us." He didn't look at her when he spoke.

"Did you see anything? Please tell me it isn't more refugees." Lena knew there had to be more people moving their way, but she'd hoped they would head past the farm.

"No. Aron said the others are waiting in a camp a day toward Crystal. There's almost a thousand people. He knows we can't accommodate any more than these."

That information was a relief and an opening. "We can't accommodate any of them. Do you know this Aron guy? Can you talk to him? Find out what they want me to do? I'm willing to help within reason. We can't support even this few through winter."

"They want our help, Lena. You seem to understand what

that means for everyone else. Even people who stole from you. Why can't you figure out what they need?"

She looked over her shoulder to the living room. Mahir was not in sight, hopefully not in earshot either. He was still sensitive about taking the supplies. With his sister Pallavi off in Prosperity, he acted like it was his job to atone no matter how many times, or how many people said it wasn't necessary.

"Well, you are still here," she said. "I guess I don't send everyone who shows up uninvited away."

"But I'm your husband, no matter what you're doing with Scott. We are still married." He reached for her hand. "I still love you."

She couldn't go down that road again. Brian would eventually give up — she hoped.

"It's going to be too late to send them on their way soon," she said. "They only have a few months of clear traveling time. If I can't get them to move on soon, they'll be here for the winter. We can't feed them, and we can't let them die on our doorstep."

"So you do care about something."

"Of course I fucking care," she yelled before getting control of her temper. "Sorry. Look, Brian, it seems to me like they feel entitled to help. I didn't cause their problems; I can't solve any of them. The world is different, and they need to change. The people who survive are the ones who learn to live with what's available."

"They know that," Brian said. "You treat them like sulky teenagers."

And that's how they act. "I need you to talk to Aron. He's some kind of leader. Banging on my door and demanding help isn't getting us anywhere. Find out exactly what they want and if I can give it, I will."

"So, I'm an ambassador? Just for these refugees, or for everyone who comes by?"

Always looking for status. It couldn't hurt to give him the title. No power came with the job, but he'd feel like he was important. "You would be good at it. But any decisions or negotiations come back to the group. Okay?"

"Of course. I'll see what I can do." He finished the muffin and left her in the kitchen.

Maybe Aron could be convinced that Brian would be an asset. This might solve two problems. In fact, maybe in the next couple of days, the refugees would be gone with Brian, and the farm would be peaceful again. Scott and Tik would decide exploring in spring would be better and maybe dinner could be a celebration.

She checked the bread bin and then collected the ingredients to replenish the supply. Since Prosperity had built the mill, they had flour that didn't need picking over for non-edible components.

Mellow stepped in and offered to help. "Tik spoke to you, right? About his plans."

"To explore, with Scott? You don't mind?" There was really nothing she could do to stop them. But a delay might be possible.

"I'm fine. There's been something I want to do that... well, I need some time without him hanging around."

It was difficult being together all the time. Lena was so involved in Brian's annoying behavior she forgot the need for some alone time. Going for a long walk didn't always work. You had to be careful of nature because she often bit you in the ass.

"Is everything okay with you two?"

"Oh, yeah. I have plans of my own." She looked up from kneading bread dough. "We need a school. I want to build it. Not just for us, but for kids from all the communities. Mixing up the kids will make the alliance stronger."

A project was exactly what they needed. "Where are you thinking?"

Mellow patted the dough into a ball and set it aside to proof. "I thought if we built a new barn, we could put dormitories on a second level and classes on the ground floor. The kids can work on the farm for part of their classes."

It was good for kids to form bonds. "Redstone, Crystal, and Prosperity all have schools. Why would they send kids here?"

"Not just kids, teachers too. Because it's more effective. We can agree on a curriculum and everyone gets the same chance to learn. We all bring different skills to teach. We offer the farm and hunting; Prosperity has some manufacturing."

It was the first Lena had heard of the school project, but maybe Mellow had talked to Ava. She'd certainly thought the whole thing through. "Draw up a proposal we can take to the other communities. Lesson plan, timing, curriculum."

Mellow smiled and agreed.

The world is changing again.

CHAPTER FOUR

Mellow had been gone only a moment when Brian came back. "I have an idea."

There was no way he found the real problem so quickly, Lena thought. "What do they want?" She steeled herself for bad news.

He shook his head as though her ideas were less important. "I didn't go to the camp. I thought about what I would need. I think we can get them to move on if we help them be successful."

"No kidding, Brian. I asked you to find out what that means to them." Things were moving too fast. All Lena wanted was a moment to digest the changes that would come without Scott and Tik, and with a barn full of school kids. She let the thought go and focused on Brian's words. "Did you even consider that what they want might be something different from what you want? Not everyone has the same dreams."

"You could at least hear me out." He didn't actually pout, but Lena recognized the signs.

"Okay, what would you want?"

Brian gestured to the chair, inviting her to sit. He was acting more like he was the head of the farm. Lena wanted the conversation over and Brian in the camp finding a solution. She pulled out a chair across from where Brian stood.

"Obviously they need a place to settle, and someone who knows how to survive in this kind of situation. If I were them, I'd want you to point me in the right direction and send along a guide or two."

If he was going to simply state the obvious, Lena would scream. He couldn't even follow through on a simple request; his idea was the same as Tik and Scott's. She wouldn't put it past him to have listened at the window. It was definitely time for him to find a new home.

"I don't own the country," she said. "We haven't explored enough to find them a city to take over. And it's not our job to decide who settles where."

Brian smiled. "But we do own maps, Lena. We know even if people are living in a town, they need more bodies. That's why the smaller places failed. When people like you ran off, we didn't have enough left to keep the farms going, keep the police strong. You knew that; you just didn't care."

"It would have happened whether I stayed or not."

He tensed but took control before he lashed out like he usually did. "Yes. Do you want to hear my idea or not? I think if we go to the camp with a plan, they will accept it. You are asking them for something they can't give you. They are still in shock and tired of trying to live a life they aren't prepared for. The Lena I loved would understand that."

He didn't know me even then. She refused to engage in a nostalgic discussion of a time that never really existed.

"You think they don't have a clue what they want?" As much as he annoyed her, Brian lived their life and faced the same challenges. He knew what made the power structure of a city work. He might well be right. "What's the plan?"

"They can make Calgary in two or three months. A good place to wait out the winter if it is still occupied."

And there were places along the way that might suit them better and were more likely to be empty. "It's a long way if they need help," Lena said.

"I thought you wanted them gone?"

"I do." She waved him to silence and for the first time in her memory he sat back and waited for her to think it through. At some undefined distance she didn't need to worry about helping these people get settled. How far was that? Even the couple of days between the alliance communities made it hard to be responsive to a call for assistance. Going as far as Calgary would make them someone else's problem, and it was close enough that anyone could make it given enough time. "It might take them closer to six months."

"Yes, but they'd make it to Regina before it's too late." He smiled and Lena knew he assumed she would agree.

It was a good plan. And one that applied to every group that passed through, especially if this group left markers along their path.

"Okay, so we send them that way. We should be able to give them a route to follow. The roads are still good for foot and wagon travel. What about survival skills? Who goes to teach them?"

"Scott," Brian said. "No. It's not what you think. He survived long before you met up. He knows the road; he knows how to hunt. He isn't much use on the farm until he gets strong again, and the trip will help him with that."

And he wants to explore.

Keith walked into the kitchen as Lena tried to find the words that would send Brian instead of Scott. "Lena, we need to talk about security. I don't like the way the people in the camp feel like they can wander around the farm."

"We were talking. Do you mind waiting?" Brian said.

The words took away any doubts Lena had about Brian leaving. He did have skills, but not ones useful on the farm, or anywhere without levels of status to manipulate.

"We're almost done," she said. "Brian, I think you should go with them when they leave. I'll talk to Scott about the rest of it, but you can help them settle in their new location."

He glared at her, but Lena turned to Keith.

"They'll be gone soon. Is there a temporary solution?"

Keith glanced at Brian and then sat. Brian marched out of the room and Lena found she didn't care where he was going.

"Problems?" Keith asked.

"Nothing new. He'll be going with the refugees if I need to gag him and tie him to a horse. Now what about the security?"

"You think they'll go?"

Lena nodded.

"Then we can keep an eye on them. Don't want to find the stores empty after they leave."

There was something more. Lena waited. If Keith was done, he'd leave. It was unusual for him not to just say what was on his mind.

"Deb said I should talk to you."

"Sickness? Do we need quarantine?" *Will there ever be a time when I won't have to solve someone's huge problem.*

"No. We want to set up our own homestead. A small holding and a butcher shop."

Was everyone except Brian eager to leave? "I can't persuade you to stay?"

"No. We want to set up our own home. We won't go until you're settled with this situation, and we won't go more than a half day away. There's the perfect place just north of the farm. We need to be near customers." He smiled and leaned in. "Lena, it's not about anything but us wanting something of ours. Deb will still be the nurse; she'll keep teaching people."

Brian isn't the only one who needs reminding about different dreams. How many of us really want to stay on the farm?

"I understand. We'll help you set up. Thanks for sticking around until we have our land back."

Maybe when everyone leaves, I should invite more people to the farm, people who want to stay. Two new couples, or two single people would be fine. She had to count on Scott and Tik coming back, but neither had their own room anyway.

Mellow's school would be a great new interest, one that might fill the gap. The farm work was getting easier with the new plows and harvesters that Prosperity had devised. She grabbed a glass and filled it with whiskey. She usually took her drink to the porch after dinner, but right now she felt the need for her evening ritual.

The sun hadn't quite set but fires were glowing from the camp. Another reason for sitting on the porch every evening: she got a good look at the number of people. Inside, with only the problems to occupy her, the camp grew in her imagination to fill the horizon.

A horse approached. Unusual for this late in the day. She saw the bright yellow saddlebags of the post. JC would be welcome to spend the night.

"Lena," JC called out as he slowed his horse to a walk then came to a stop, "got some mail for you. From Prosperity."

"You can put the horse in the stable. One of the kids will groom her so you don't need to."

"No time. I'm overnighting an hour down the road. Got me a sweetheart."

He dug into the bag and handed her a sheet of paper sealed with a wax blob.

"Probably more than one. A good-looking guy like you

must be drowning in girlfriends," Lena said as she took the letter.

"They don't mind sharing, and they all know about the others. Sometimes write letters to each other. New world, new rules," he said. "Anything for me to take?"

Lena shook her head. The mail was reliable but not fast enough. A full circuit could take two weeks. Lena preferred to visit rather than wait for JC to make it around. It was only a couple of days each way.

JC waved goodbye as he turned his horse to get back to the road. "You expecting more people?" he asked.

"I didn't expect these," Lena said. "They should be gone soon."

"Make sure they don't block the road. I'm not fighting through a crowd to deliver," he said as he turned his horse and rode away.

The letter was addressed to the farm but not anyone in particular, so Lena broke the seal. Pallavi's writing.

Nothing big in the way of news, but she was on her way to visit. Mahir would be happy to see her. He'd missed his sister when she went to Prosperity.

Lena tossed back the last of the whiskey and returned to the house, calling Mahir as she closed the door behind her.

CHAPTER FIVE

"No!" Mahir yelled after Lena told him about the visit.

Not the reaction she expected at all. "She's probably on her way. And I would never tell her not to come to see us."

"She wants to take me to Prosperity. I know it." He screwed up his face in anger.

Lena took his hand, afraid he would run away to avoid talking, like he often did. When he came to them almost a year ago, he was a malnourished ten-year-old grieving his father's death and Pallavi's abduction by Newton Cole's men. Today, he was a normal little boy, always into something and in need of a nighttime story. Unlike most kids his age, his moods swung wildly. Bev said it was trauma and he could take a long time to heal.

"Why don't you want to go if that's what Pallavi wants? Don't you think you should be together?"

"I like living here. She can stay at the farm. We can be a family here," he muttered.

But Pallavi had more of a future in Prosperity. So did Mahir. He did his share of the work without complaining, but

Lena always thought he saw it as a game, and that he'd rather be learning things, becoming someone more than a farmer; not that there were many jobs that didn't focus on food and safety. Farmer or some kind of soldier were the main choices.

"You can visit us," she said. It wasn't her job to come between family members. "Anyway, maybe she's coming back for some other reason." If she could stop his worrying about leaving, he'd look forward to Pallavi's visit. And it did feel good that one person was fighting to stay with her.

Everyone was here because they wanted to be. Scott and Tik hadn't really asked her permission to go. And she would have told them they were free agents no matter how much she wanted to keep them with her by saying no.

"No. She told me when she left that she'd come back to get me when she was settled. She loves Evan and he won't live here."

He had tears in his eyes and Lena knew they weren't all from frustration.

"He would be welcome." She would much rather have Evan around than Brian, but that didn't mean much.

"He won't. My friends are here. I don't know anyone in Prosperity. My dad is buried here." He pulled his hand away and ran upstairs.

A scared and angry child is the perfect end to a difficult day.

Lena considered hiding out in farm work and letting someone else deal with these problems. She didn't try because she knew they would hunt her out no matter where she hid.

Dinner prep was a good way to push away her fretting. The small motions of peeling vegetables and watching pots relaxed Lena. Ava stood beside her, preparing meat for the stew.

"Should we offer to feed the refugees?" Ava asked.

"They have their own food. God knows where they found it. I thought the stores were all scavenged clean a year ago."

"Probably best not to ask," Ava said. "And I guess they would take it as an invitation to stay."

"They seem to think I can come up with a plan for their future." Lena added the vegetable peelings to the compost bucket. "I hate to prove them right, but I talked to Scott about escorting them west."

"Jason is getting restless," Ava said. "He wants to go exploring. I want to hold on to him as long as I can."

Her son was in his early teens, no wonder he was itching for his own adventure. "Did he say anything? Or is this you anticipating a problem?"

"He's talking about going with Tik and Scott. He says he needs to know what's out there." She tossed the meat chunks into the pan. "He's only just turned thirteen."

Logic wasn't going to help. She didn't say the words aloud, but Ava was struggling. Knowing that thirteen these days was almost an adult didn't put her at ease. Lena understood kids from her time as a teacher, but not having her own sometimes got in the way of saying the right thing. "Do you expect him to stick around here forever?"

Ava poked at the ingredients in the pan. "Yes, but I know it's not going to happen. We need farmers to stay with us; Jason isn't that. But I'm not ready. If Jason goes, Maya might not be far behind."

Everyone wanted to go. How was Lena going to keep the farm running alone? Would Keith and Deb stay if they could have the farm? "She's young enough to want to be here with you. And she has Mahir to hang out with."

"But in a few years, she'll be looking for a partner. Mahir isn't going to fit in that mold, he's too young." Ava transferred the meat from the pan to the soup pot and added onions.

"We don't have any unattached men here, or girls if that's what she wants."

It wasn't just Maya who would need to find someone. Ava was still young enough to want another relationship. This wasn't going away, and Lena needed to figure out a long-term plan rather than assuming life would continue as it was. "What about you?" she asked. "If it comes down to me and Scott here, will you go too?"

Ava shrugged as she added water to the pot. "I could always bring someone back here. It's not like we're going to abandon the farm."

It feels to me like that's exactly what is happening.

"We need a meeting," Lena said. "Before everyone takes off."

It felt like the farm was unraveling and she couldn't stop it. But she wouldn't try to hold them here either.

"It has been a while since we had a family meeting," Ava said.

"I get that you're worried," Lena said. "But Scott and Tik will look out for Jason. Isn't it better to send him with your blessing than let him run after them later?"

"It's falling apart, right?" Ava asked. "Something changed this spring. We're restless and on the verge of screwing everything up."

"You were never such a drama queen," Lena said, laughing to take the edge off the words. "Scott and Tik will come back. Jason too. How come the only person I would love to see go is so willing to stick around?"

Ava chuckled. "Maybe Brian is the thing that changed. Don't worry, you'll figure out how to move him along."

"The school will help," Lena said. "Mellow's project might just be enough to get us over the boredom, or at least the waiting time."

"And we should check with the refugees," Ava said. "Maybe there are some budding farmers in the camp. People we want to keep here."

"I doubt it," Lena said. Before they offered a place at the farm for anyone, Lena wanted a firm agreement the rest of the refugees would leave, and soon.

CHAPTER SIX

The day was finally coming to an end. Lena rested her hip on the porch rail and watched the refugee camp quiet down for the night. Tomorrow she would make them leave. She remembered when her group had turned up at the farm, starving and desperate enough to consider killing the occupants to get a place to live. These people had tents and food and clothing. They hadn't lost anything to a monster like Abigail or had to kill a predator to protect a child. They would never understand what that did to you. Tomorrow she'd see them off, even if it took a show of force.

"Everyone is turning in," Scott said, bringing the jug of homemade whiskey with him as he joined her.

"I'm not that far behind. It's been a long day. Too many people want to leave the farm."

"We're not leaving forever," Scott said, wrapping his arm around her shoulders. "I talked to Ava. We'll take Jason if she lets him come."

"I don't think she has a choice." Lena let Scott refill her glass. "He's not too young, right?"

"If he is, he won't make it far. I'll make sure he comes

home if that's the right thing. But you didn't think the kids would stay forever, did you?"

"I hadn't really thought about it. They are still young to me."

"What's Brian going to do?" Scott asked the question Lena dreaded.

"I want him to go with the refugees," she said. "Although it's a harder sell than I expected."

"I can't believe you married him."

"The Brian I married was a different man. I was different too. We all were." Scott stiffened with the effort of keeping his opinion inside. Lena reached up to touch his arm. "I can't go back to that person. I don't care what Brian wants. I don't want him."

"That's not why I'm leaving. I need some space. Lena, I went from being on the road alone to being with you so fast it didn't feel like a choice."

"Are you sure you aren't leaving because our relationship has run its course?"

Scott downed his drink. "I didn't think it had. You tell me you don't want to get back with Brian, but I have a hard time believing it when you say things like that."

She didn't know how to solve this. They weren't communicating any longer, just pushing at each other's insecurities. Scott wouldn't admit that he was jealous of Brian, partly because of all the time he'd spent recovering from the wound in the fight with Newton Cole's men left him feeling weak. She couldn't bring herself to admit that she was terrified for him out there if he left: that he would get hurt and die, that she would never see him again. Brian being an ass made things worse because she couldn't get past the feeling Scott's feelings were all about jealousy. It stopped him from saying the important things.

Things she couldn't express either, like *I love you, I need you, please stay here.*

"I don't want what we have to end. I only said it because I thought you wanted an out."

"I'm not Brian. If I wanted out, I'd tell you. I don't hang around where I'm not wanted." He picked up the jug and marched back into the house.

The liquid in Lena's glass was vibrating with the tension of her grasp. Now she had no way to talk to Scott without running after him, and she didn't trust her temper enough to do it.

It was all slipping away from her; her peaceful life, Scott, the future. The camp suddenly felt more like a threat than an annoyance. The farm was never heavily defended, but in a couple of days they would lose so many people that it would be easy pickings. Maybe she should have asked JC to take a letter asking for help.

The night didn't bring Lena any relief. Scott had slept on the sofa, so no opportunity to rectify the arguments and misunderstandings. And the damn refugees were still camped out front. Not that she'd expected them to disappear in the night.

No. She would focus on the farm and her family for a while. It was time for a planning session for Mellow's school. Mahir and Maya were sitting at the table because Mellow thought they would have some good input. Lena didn't agree but would be happy to be wrong.

Someone knocked at the door. Lena wasn't in the mood for an emissary demanding action. "Mahir, can you go check who that is?"

He jumped up and grabbed his notes. "No. It's Pallavi and I won't go with her." He ran upstairs before anyone could say that it was too soon for his sister to arrive and that she would come in, not knock.

Sighing, Lena sent Maya after the boy and went to see what new problem required her, and only her, to fix.

On the porch stood a small woman with the pale skin usually associated with chronic under-nourishment, limp, dirty blond hair, and bowed shoulders.

"What do you want?" Lena asked. There was no need to encourage anyone from the camp with politeness.

"Have you found God again? Are you ready to repent for the sins that brought on the plagues?" She held out a sheet of paper filled with handwritten paragraphs.

The words didn't match the almost dead look in the woman's eyes. If she believed, wouldn't she show some passion? Some fervor? Was she just parroting some script?

Lena stepped back and didn't reach for the paper. "The plagues happened because people made stupid, selfish decisions."

"My name is Faith."

Why did she think that was important? "We aren't interested. You can see there are more people here than we can support. Can God find them a home?"

"We all live on this planet," Faith said. Her voice didn't change from the quiet monotone. "Our homes are where our bodies rest."

"No. Our homes are where we work to grow food and build shelter and create community," Lena said despite wanting to slam the door and let the world get on without her help.

"We all have different blessings. Yours is to build this wonderful home. Mine is to create a home for the soul."

The soul needed the body and the body needed food and shelter. Why did this Faith think otherwise?

"You are wasting your time here," Lena said as she pulled the door to close it.

Faith smiled as though Lena had agreed with her, but her hand reached for the door to stop it closing. "Perhaps, but there are others inside who may wish to talk to me."

Lena didn't answer. If anyone inside wanted to hear Faith's world-view, she didn't know her people at all. She pulled the door free and shut out the world.

CHAPTER SEVEN

"We'll take Jason," Scott said. They were standing on the porch surveying the camp.

"What?" Lena wondered where they would take him. Then her mind caught up. Jason was going scouting too.

Their fight from yesterday was over. They didn't fight often because Scott was awful at dealing with the fallout. Lena had become used to just letting things go unless there was something important burning to be resolved. Their relationship was important, but this time it could wait.

"I know Ava said he could go, but I told Jason he had to get his mom's okay. If he can't do that, he isn't ready for the road. And I wasn't going to stand between Ava and her kid."

"And Tik?" They were going whether she liked it or not. She might as well get on board with the idea.

"He's okay with it. Jason knows what it's like on the road. He is a good kid and he's old enough to come with us. We have a plan." Scott wrapped her in a hug. "We'll take the refugees off your hands and settle them somewhere. We'll go in the morning so we can travel all day. Mahir said he'd join us."

She looked up at him. Scott was grinning.

"He thinks he can avoid Pallavi so she can't take him to Prosperity," he added. "The kid is persistent; you have to give him credit for that."

"I doubt he's given thought to life on the road," Lena said. "He came here in a car before things went totally off-track."

"He learns fast."

"He's not coming with you even if we have to lock him in his room." She leaned back into Scott's arms. "I'll miss you." Lena was already thinking she had a day to make Brian go with them. It would have to be enough. "How long will you be gone, do you think?"

He pulled her inside to sit on the couch. "I don't really want to spend the winter on the road, but if we take the refugees as far as they can go, we won't have a lot of choices. We can't afford to be caught in the mountains, but we thought we'd go south and then head back. We can move pretty fast without a crowd. So, shortly after the first snows?"

It was long enough to get a good idea about the settled part of their world. Surely some communities continued. "How far south?"

"Far enough that we'll know if there's a point to going out next year or not."

Lena wiggled out of his arms. "How often are you planning to desert me?"

He reached for her. "I'm not deserting you, woman. We need to explore and do it often. It might not be me next time. With some preliminary scouting, we can work with Crystal and Redstone to send out groups."

His words made sense to her, but Lena couldn't hide the fear that he wouldn't come back. "What did Deb say about you traveling? Are you strong enough?"

He squeezed her and kissed the top of her head. "I'm fit. I

know it took months, but I'm fine. Look, you'll get a report from Jason. We agreed that he would turn back when we knew where the refugees were settling. He's capable of making a few weeks journey by himself, don't worry."

"Ava won't like that." Lena sighed. "That's not my problem until he's gone. We will have our hands full with the school."

"And Brian."

So, he hasn't forgotten the argument.

She turned to look at him and grinned. "Oh, he's going with you. I'm not letting you dump that problem on me. And besides, he'll be of use to a new community."

Scott let her go and stood. "Let's hope he's useful to them on the road. I'm not carrying his sorry ass all the way across the country."

"As far as I'm concerned, you can drop him in the nearest river." She needed to talk to Aron Simons. As the spokesperson for the camp, he should be happy to take on Brian and do his part to convince him how important he would be. By this time tomorrow, she'd be watching the last of the campers head out and have her land to herself again.

CHAPTER EIGHT

Everything was ready for the city refugees to move on. Only a couple of last-minute details to finalize. Except one big detail: Brian. If she didn't get him to agree to go now, it would be too late.

He'd disappeared after the last argument, but this time she wasn't going to wait for him to decide to show up. She began the search in his room, but he wasn't there and no clue leading to his location. The fields she could see from the house were empty, and if she couldn't find him close to home, Lena would head out to the hills, but first the outbuildings.

The root cellar they used to store food was her biggest worry. If he was in there, it would not be to make sure the stores were still good. She slipped inside and waited for her eyes to adjust to the dimness. The space wasn't much bigger than the first floor of the farmhouse, but all the shelves broke it up and created hiding places. She walked the aisles, touching a crate or barrel occasionally and sniffing the air for any hint of rot. It smelled of earth blended with the sweetness of vegetables.

Brian wasn't inside. The barn was the only other place he

could be. Lena wondered what he would find to do inside, where the air was dusty from the hay stored above the stalls, and ripe with the odor of animal droppings.

She slid the door aside enough to get through and closed it behind her. It wasn't bright, but the roof vents were letting enough light through to show Brian standing at Starbuck's stall, feeding the horse a piece of cut apple.

"He's getting greedy," she said, joining them. "We should exercise him more."

"Scott isn't taking him?" Brian asked, stroking the horse's nose.

"He's too old," Lena said. "He's earned his rest here. Do you give him treats often?"

He grinned at her and Lena saw a shadow of the Brian she fell in love with so long ago. "Just enough to get him to like me," he said. "I've always loved horses. I should probably learn to ride better. I figured bribing them would help when it came time to climb on."

So, he does have an ulterior motive. At least this time it's a smart one.

"We need to talk," she said.

"I know. I won't pretend I don't still love you." His shoulders slumped. "I'll accept that you don't feel the same."

It will be easier for him to keep his promise if he's away from me.

Starbuck stretched his neck to nudge Lena for a treat. She rubbed his nose and stepped back. "Thank you, but that's not what why I'm here, Brian. It's about the refugees."

"They are going. What else do you want?" His peaceful mood slipped away. Starbuck snuffled and stomped his hooves.

Lena pulled Brian away from the stall so the horse wouldn't react more to his emotions.

"You should go with them," she said. When Brian opened his mouth to argue, she held up her hand to forestall his knee jerk reaction. "Hear me out. They need your skills. You are good at managing groups of people. There are enough of them that you won't have to do manual work. A while on the road and then you'll be where you are meant to be, in a city."

He closed his lips around his response.

If he is willing to give it some thought, there's hope.

After a few moments, Brian nodded his head as if he'd just won an argument with himself. "You mean if I stay, you will force me to be a farmer."

It sounded harsh, but he was right. "There is only farm work here," she said. "So, if you stay, that's what you'll have to learn."

"And you don't think I can?" There was no fight in his words, just a request for an answer.

Lena took a moment. She didn't think he would do it, which was different from could. "Anyone can learn to dig, plant, harvest, and hunt. I don't think you are willing to learn. And I don't think you should. This is an opportunity for you to live the kind of life you want."

He looked around the barn. She knew he was judging what he saw; hay, horses, dirt, tools for making more dirt or cleaning up, or grooming the horses.

"I can't deny it, physical work isn't my thing. Maybe I've just been hanging on because I thought I could win you back. If that's not possible, I guess there's nothing for me on the farm."

In the hope of getting the camp broken up as early as possible, Lena had pulled everyone into the preparations. The three travelers needed food and tents and other supplies that hadn't been looked at since they'd unpacked on arrival.

Brian had reluctantly agreed to go; he was off sulking, as

though waiting out the departure so she couldn't force the issue.

The tents were set to air out; fortunately no holes eaten by bugs or vermin showed up. The bedrolls, on the other hand, were ruined by mold, so Mellow and Deb were sewing some extra blankets into replacements. Keith and Maya, with Mahir's help, were packing trail food to supplement whatever could be hunted or foraged.

In the midst of this, Ava was instructing Jason on everything from hygiene to first aid — all things Jason knew well enough. He was patient. A level of maturity that boded well for his success on the road.

"Maybe I should go along, too," Mahir said. "That way Pallavi can't take me away. And I'll be a lot of help."

Nice try, kid.

"We need you here," Ava said before Lena could chime in. "We won't have many people to help with the farm when they leave."

Mahir brightened. "Maybe Pallavi should stay here, too."

"It's up to her," Lena said. "She has made a life in Prosperity. I think the farm brings her too many memories."

He tucked a small sack of dried fruit into one of the saddlebags and gave it a pat. "Just so I don't have to go. I like it here."

Lena figured it was better to let the conversation die at that point. If Pallavi wanted to take Mahir, there wasn't much anyone could do about it. And Ava had stepped in as his surrogate parent, so she'd deal with any problems. If he went, she'd miss him.

"Mom, I have to go pack my stuff and check my horse," Jason said in a pause between instructions. He didn't wait for her to react, just hustled out the front door.

"I'm being nuts, right?" Ava asked. "Maybe it will pass when he's gone. Like I'll still worry, but I won't exactly know what to worry about? Parents did it for generations before me." She pulled a face that made Lena chuckle.

"Scott and Tik will take care of him. Neither of them wants to come back to face you otherwise." Lena finished patching a tear in Scott's shirt and folded it for packing. It was hard to keep things in perspective. She didn't want him to go, but he was an adult, and he was experienced.

She turned at the knock on the front door and found herself wishing for the days when no one visited. She noticed Mahir run out the back, still convinced that his sister was going to arrive any moment and drag him away.

Not Pallavi and Evan, Aron Simons.

"Is there a problem?" Lena asked. She ushered him into the frantic living room. "You did agree to head out at first light."

"Yes. All we wanted was direction and you've given us that. Thank you. I have some news that you should hear before we go."

"Would you like some tea?" Ava asked. They were all more willing to be sociable now that departure was imminent.

"Like you, we're busy preparing. I won't take too long."

Lena watched him closely, still not sure she could trust him to go. This might be a scouting visit to see what their weaknesses were. *For crying out loud, they don't want the farm. Relax.*

"What's the news?" she asked.

"These followers of the prophet Poorjohn. You know about them?"

"Religious guy looking for a congregation?" Lena asked. "One came by yesterday and I sent her away."

"Faith. She didn't go far. When we're gone, you'll notice a few tents left behind. I promise you they aren't ours."

Weariness flooded her at the thought. "Am I substituting one campground for another?"

"They are being ostracized by the residents of the camp. I'm afraid they plan to stay but can't be sure. At least there are only a few of them. You should be able to deal with the problem quickly."

And just how did he think they would 'deal' with the problem? He was right about one thing; his group showed up in one giant crowd. It must be easier to deal with a few stragglers before the problem got out of hand. "Thanks for the warning."

"Pleasure. To be honest, I didn't want you chasing after us and threatening to take the guides away." He laughed. "It's been a pleasure living on your lawn, so to speak, but we're not cut out for rural life. I'm looking forward to a roof over my head and a grocery store."

She doubted their destination would have a thriving retail sector, but kept it to herself. Their future was not her problem.

"Travel safely," she said. "I remember how difficult it was when we came here. At least the world has settled a bit now."

Aron wished her well and left them to return to his activities of preparing the camp to leave.

CHAPTER NINE

The day felt as long as a week. Lena found herself reluctant for it to end, because she would say goodbye to Scott, but eager for the morning because the refugees would be gone.

The morning would bring more work for everyone with three of their family missing. But work would make the time pass.

Footsteps on the porch pulled her attention away from fretting over things she couldn't control. If anyone had come up with a reason to delay, she would scream.

It was Mischa, Redstone's head teacher. "Come in," she said. "Are you staying the night?" It was pretty late for him to set out beyond the farm.

"If you have the room," he said. He'd been a teacher in the old world too. New to the job, and good looking enough to draw a few crushes from his students. His blond curls were longer now, and his deep blue eyes carried worry that aged him.

"Always." Lena called for someone to make up the spare room. Once she would have called it a walk-in closet, but it held a bed and a lamp.

"I'm on my way to Crystal," Mischa said. "We're trying to figure out a standard curriculum that makes sense for the future. No one really needs computer skills anymore, but maybe a time will come when they do. And architecture, and..." He chuckled. "You don't need to hear my wish list."

Lena drew him to the kitchen and offered a plate of dinner leftovers. "Mellow is planning a boarding school. You should talk to her before you leave."

"I wish we had the luxury to send all the kids to one of those, but none of us can spare the labor." He tucked into the meal.

"Talk to her anyway," Lena said. "Ava and I will help her out. I kind of miss lesson planning and teaching."

"Your guests are still here, I see." He tilted his head toward the front of the farm.

"Gone tomorrow. You might want to head out before first light to avoid the crowds. Or you are welcome to stay another day if you can." Having him around might make it seem less abandoned.

"I'll go before them," he said. "If I wait, I'll just run into the back of the group at some point. I have some information you might find interesting."

News was always welcome, and if Mischa was here overnight, it could be discussed not simply reported.

"Why don't we all get together for a drink when you are settled? Everyone will want to contribute to the topic."

"You should hear this first," Mischa said. "You know about Elijah Poorjohn?"

"Just today. One of his followers knocked on the door. I sent her on her way."

"Did you make sure she left?" Mischa took his plate to the sink and cleaned it as they talked.

"Apparently, she settled in with the camp. I'm hoping she'll leave with them. More people to try to convert."

"Make sure she does. This guy is a fanatic, Lena. He set up outside Redstone a week ago. Not everyone disagreed with his message."

"No one here will buy his crap."

"I thought that too. It's not the life I want, half-starved and relying on a nutjob to feed and shelter me. But some did. Hard to understand, but people have always been that way."

Brian joined them before Mischa could comment further. "I heard we had a visitor," he said.

Lena introduced them and asked Brian to bring the rest of the family together for a drink.

"You were talking about our latest Bible thumper," Brian said, not leaving them.

Why can't he just once do as I ask? "We'll talk about it when everyone is together."

"Now, I can't leave in the morning," he said. "If this guy is headed to the farm, we must show we are strong."

"You agreed to leave with them," Lena said, keeping as much of her frustration out of her voice as she could. No need for Mischa to witness her problems.

"I changed my mind. You need all the men you can find here now. I can always go to them later. When they are settled."

When the hard work is done, more likely.

"We did fine without your help up to now," she said quietly. "How can I trust anything you say if you do this kind of thing?"

"I changed my mind because you let most of the men go," Brian said.

"You should go. You will be much happier in a town. You hate farm work, and we will always be just that." *Please don't do this.*

"We can talk later," Brian said. "I'll get everyone together." He walked out as if it was his idea.

"Sorry," Lena said. "You didn't need to see that."

Mischa grinned. "I've seen more of that kind of behavior than you'd expect. It seems without a threat like Cole, some people fall back into resentment that their old life is gone."

"It's been gone a long time," Lena said.

"He's right about needing a show of force," Mischa said. "You need to discourage Poorjohn if he comes."

"I'm not starting a fight," she said. "Maybe he isn't coming to us. I mean, there are only a handful of us. Why wouldn't he just go on to Crystal, or keep going, or even try to convert the refugees?"

"He's a fanatic, Lena. And you are in the middle of some pretty large communities for these times. Don't forget how important your position on the road is."

"We'll deal with it if he comes," she said. "I don't have the resources to do anything else. The farm needs us to be working, not preparing for problems that might not come."

"The alliance needs clear roads and peaceful trade," Mischa said. "Don't wait too long to ask for help. I'm betting Poorjohn knows exactly the importance of holding the farm. He talks a good game about God and service to everyone, but he's hungry for something more than a humble life."

"I hope not," Lena said. "I will be careful. And you promise you'll do the same. Let Crystal know about the city refugees passing through and that we might need some assistance from them."

He promised and headed out for a cigarette.

CHAPTER TEN

Mischa's decision to leave at first light turned out to be smart. Only an hour later and the scene was a riot of action, a stark contrast to the previous weeks. As Lena watched the camp organize to leave, she had a more optimistic view of their plan. Yesterday, this had seemed a petulant crowd of entitled idiots. Today, she was far more certain they'd make it. If only Brian was here to witness the chaos, perhaps he would be persuaded at the last minute to leave too, because only he could organize them.

"Jason, you listen to Scott and Tik. You don't take risks and you come back, no matter what." Ava held her son's shoulders and stared him in the eyes. He was so tall now, she looked up to do that.

"Mom, I know how to take care of myself," his embarrassment evident in his tone and his flushed cheeks. "I won't do anything stupid."

Lena watched the struggle on Ava's face. She didn't want to make a scene. She was proud of her son and mortally afraid he would die on the trail.

"I'm sorry we fought," Scott said to Lena, wrapping her in an embrace. "I know you can deal with Brian."

"And you're glad not to have him annoying you on this trip," she said into his shoulder. "Don't be surprised if he shows up in a few days. I plan to make his life hell."

He kissed the top of her head. "Give us a week, please?" A chuckle punctuated the words.

Lena hugged him back and then let him go. "No. If I can get rid of him, I'm not waiting. He's trouble and not just for us."

"They are ready," Tik interrupted the conversation. "We should go to the head of the group."

Mellow wasn't here to say goodbye. Lena hoped it was because the couple had said their goodbyes privately, not because they parted on bad terms.

"Okay, let's go." Mahir strode out to the porch dressed in jeans and tee-shirt with sneakers on his feet and an old canvas backpack hanging from his shoulder. "We shouldn't waste the day."

Mahir was deadly serious. Lena fought to keep from laughing. She saw the same in the other adults around her. "I thought you were staying with us," she said.

"No. I said I am going. You can't stop me," he said with determination. "The only one who gets to order me around is Pallavi, and she's not here."

"She will be soon," Ava said. "But if you're determined to go, I think you need a bit more in the way of supplies."

"What?" He patted his backpack. "I have food, clean clothes and underwear, and some snacks and water."

"What are you going to sleep on?" Scott asked. "And are you going to walk?"

His sureness wavered. "I can sleep on the ground. And I will fit on Jason's horse."

"You'll get sick if you sleep on the ground," Ava said. She

turned back to the house. "Maya, see if we have another bedroll to spare for Mahir."

It was cruel to play along, but it was better than fighting. And he'd simply run off as soon as their backs were turned if they didn't convince him to see reason.

Maya stepped out with a bedroll under her arm and pendant on a chain in her hand. "This is for Jason," she said, holding up the pendant. "A Saint Christopher medallion. He's supposed to protect travelers."

"Thanks, sis," Jason said, putting it on.

She held out the bedroll to Mahir. "I'm going to be the only kid here now."

"I'll come back," Mahir said.

"Maybe you won't," Maya let a tear run down her cheek. "I guess I can find another friend. Maybe Pallavi will help."

Mahir swallowed.

Ava and Maya had cooked this strategy up. How had she missed the signs that the boy would try to leave? Maybe she hadn't missed the signs, just ignored them.

"It's going to be lonely here," Maya continued. "I can tell you anything is better than the road, though. Bugs will bite, and they are huge. You'll be hungry and thirsty. You have to use the outside as a bathroom. And there's no one there to help if you get hurt."

Mahir's face paled as Maya listed the facts about his great adventure. "I feel bad leaving you here," he said and then turned to Scott and Tik. "I should stay. They need me here."

"You can come another time," Scott said. "Look after the farm while we're gone?"

Mahir nodded and took his bag and bedroll inside.

The three men — it was hard to think of Jason as a boy in the circumstances — gave final farewells and mounted their horses to lead the group on the first steps of the long journey.

The camp straggled behind at first. A few tents still being

dismantled as people gained room to maneuver. Dust clouded up and obscured the progress, but Lena had no intention of returning to the house until the last refugee disappeared around the bend in the road. When that was done, there were chores and farm work to get back to.

"Why didn't we think of joining them?" Ava asked. "I just realized that was never on the table. We could still go, you know."

"Where did that come from?" Lena turned to look at her friend. "I thought you were happy here."

Ava laughed. "If I never go more than a couple of days away from here, I'll be satisfied. And I have Maya to stay for even if I had wanderlust. She's too young to leave behind."

"We'd look after her if you want to head out with them," Lena said, knowing that wasn't what Ava meant. "This is my home. As long as the rest of the world stays out there, I'm happy."

"I guess that's true for me too," Ava said. "But people are leaving. How will we run the farm? And Jason would kill me for going when I wanted him to stay."

They were responsible for the supply of produce to the allied communities. If not for that, Lena would let most of the farm go fallow and only work enough of the land to keep the family healthy. "Let them get past Crystal. Then we'll be able to talk to the other communities. I'm sure we will have a few volunteers to come live with us if it comes to that."

Ava grunted agreement. "I suppose." She pointed in the direction of the camp. "Some of them stayed."

Three tents clustered near the road. Aron had promised the city refugees would all go, and Lena believed him. "The missionaries. Well, three tents will be easy to move along."

"We should do it now," Ava said. "Send Keith and Brian to push them out. Before they start expecting us to feed them."

Lena didn't plan to encourage the intruders by sharing

their food. And she would make sure no one stole from them. They had enough people to set a small guard but that was all.

"Not today, or not right now, anyway." She opened the door and held it for Ava. "Let's just enjoy our victory over one pest before we deal with the next. They might not even stay around."

Her stomach clenched at the echo of her thoughts when the city refugees arrived. But this was different, only a few people, not a mob arriving all at once. "We'll keep people away from them. If they aren't getting traction on their recruitment efforts, I'm sure they'll move along like they've done before."

She closed the door behind Ava and glanced at the tents again. At least they stayed on the other side of the road from the farm. Still her land, but not on her doorstep.

CHAPTER ELEVEN

The next day another missionary came to convert them. Lena had no trouble turning her away; none of them were persistent. Of course, that made it harder to push back because with no resistance there was no push.

She stood on the porch watching this one wander back to the handful of tents that occupied the field across the way. A field they were currently letting go fallow. She'd planned to turn it into an alfalfa crop next season.

The camp was still small, and she hoped it would be gone soon. Surely Poorjohn would find a more productive place to recruit than this farm that now contained eight people. If they were left with no other choice, all of them could fight, but would the missionaries think that? Were they planning on the women and children being weak? Religions generally didn't give much credit to women.

The conversation inside drifted out to her.

"I don't want to learn math," Mahir said. He was growing into a stubborn boy who refused to do anything he didn't want to, and he mostly seemed to want to play. She'd given him a lot of slack because of his history, but the time had come for him to start being part of the family and not a pampered child.

"It's only a test," Mellow said. "Maya will be there."

"So, you can test just her."

"It'll be interesting," Maya said. "And when the school opens, we'll be ahead of the other kids, right?"

"We don't know," Mellow said. "But you have to learn these things anyway, Mahir."

"But I want to work on the farm," he said. "I don't need math for that."

Lena smiled at the memory of similar conversations over the years.

"If you want to be sure how much seed you need, or how long the produce will last, or how much you can safely share..." Mellow's voice became quieter and the end of the sentence didn't make it to the porch.

A better answer than Lena had ever come up with. Maybe when Pallavi came, she would help her brother settle in better to the farm, if she let him stay, or if not then to enjoy lessons in Prosperity where there was more variety. It was a lot to ask. Mahir still hurt from his experience, but Pallavi had been kidnapped and held at the fort. She'd been threatened with a life of sexual exploitation, and the man buried in the small cemetery was her father too. She was young and shouldn't be acting as the parent in the family. Perhaps Mahir could stay with them. Pallavi should be thinking about starting her own family, not trying to mother a kid like Mahir. If he stayed, Ava would have a child to fill the gap when Maya eventually sought her own future.

Without the eavesdropping to distract her, Lena's thoughts went back to defending the farm.

If Keith and Deb left, their force would be down to the bare minimum. She had no idea if Brian could fight, let alone if he would. A part of her expected him to run if things got hard. Another thing to add to her list of tasks; train Brian so he's ready to stand with them in a fight. If it wasn't Poorjohn's people, it would be someone else. Peaceful living included preparing for the worst. Defeating the fort hadn't brought an end to their enemies.

She looked out again, trying to assess the threat. Six tents now. Each holding between two and four people, so not an army. And the missionaries were grimy and on the edge of malnutrition. They didn't look like a threat.

If she only considered what she saw, Lena might just dismiss them as an irritation that would end. But too many questions picked at her. Why park themselves here? Where was their leader? And how did they communicate with the other groups scattered around the area?

Lena helped Deb roll old cotton tee-shirts into bandages.

Deb looked up at Lena and chuckled. "I know it seems never-ending, but I was taught that you never have enough dressings. Before the plagues, we always kept six months' supply on hand."

"And then when the disaster did come, no one needed bandages," Lena said. "It's good to have some use for the old sheets and towels. I hate throwing anything away these days."

Keith stood at the counter sharpening knives and arrow-heads. "I get the same way about our hunting tools. I'd love to find a hardware store like we did in Millerville. At least you can make bandages out of old sheets. I need to find a way to replace metal."

Lena added that to the long list of problems to solve when they found the time. Some of the things on the list were going to be impossible to replace. The medicine supply was almost gone. The expiry dates were long in the past, but Deb said they would do no harm; most would be weaker but still work. Even if they found a pharmacy, all those meds would be expired too.

"Will you leave us some medications when you and Keith head out?" Lena didn't know how else to open the subject of their leaving. She couldn't let that happen until things stabilized. Keith was the best fighter they had, and the best hunter. Brian was useless and Mahir too young.

"Of course. I thought we could create batches of some of the natural versions of the meds too." Deb tucked the neat roll of cloth into the box on the table between them. "We won't be that far away. I think we'll probably become a sort of clinic for the small holders as well as the farm. The towns have their own doctors."

"When will you go?" Lena asked.

"Not until this is settled," Keith said, pointing in the direction of the camp. "And if they aren't gone soon, we'll stick around until spring."

"Thank you," Lena said. "I didn't like to ask."

"You thought, after everything we've been through together, we'd abandon you?" Deb asked. She looked sincerely shocked. "I thought you knew us better than that."

"No. I wasn't sure what you planned. I trust you to do the right thing," Lena said, trying to calm the growing snit. Every time she thought Deb had changed, the woman brought out the entitled cheerleader of her youth. Even when Lena was willing to let them decide to go, Deb was offended. "I guess I didn't expect Scott or Tik to go either. I had to be sure who could help if we needed it."

"Probably won't matter," Keith said. "I don't see anyone in the camp who would pose a threat. But maybe we should practice a few skills. Haven't needed them since we defeated the fort. It's easy to let things slip."

"All of us," Lena said. Then, hearing Deb draw breath to refuse, "except Deb. We need her safe to deal with injuries."

Keith smiled behind his wife's back; he'd been with her for years, plenty of time to learn how to deal with his wife's ego. "What about Brian?"

"Definitely him." Lena wasn't going to let him sit back and watch.

"I meant, he's way behind everyone," Keith said. "The kids need a bit more refreshing than the adults. They've grown and started to develop, so they need to get used to the skills with their new bodies. But has Brian ever fought?"

She could see how it would make a difference. As an ex-teacher, she knew that a class suffered if there was too much range between the students at the top and those at the bottom. "He won't agree to learn with the kids," she said.

"He'd hold them back," Keith said.

"And get them hurt, or be hurt himself," Deb said.

"Do you have time to give him separate training?"

Keith wiped the blade he'd just honed and placed it in a sheath. He picked up the next, a machete, and started sharpening the edge in long strokes of the stone. "He needs to learn to hunt too."

He needs to leave. Lena didn't say the words aloud. This conversation was not going to become a Brian-bashing tournament. "I suppose that's true. It's his choice. If he won't leave, then he is going to learn to contribute."

"Thought I would take him out the next time I go. I can give him a lesson on one or two of the basics. Maybe he'll be good enough to join the kids then."

"I'll talk to him," Lena said. "When are you going on the next hunt?"

"A couple of days won't make much difference," Keith said, then turned his concentration back to the machete.

"Do you wonder why he hangs around?" Deb asked. "I mean, even he can see you don't want him here."

"You'd be surprised at how Brian can delude himself,"

Lena said, reaching for another strip of fabric. "I think he believes I'll take him in and give him control of the farm."

"You wouldn't though?" Deb asked, surprised.

"Never. And as soon as Scott returns, we'll both work on relieving my ex-husband of his fantasy, if he's still here and I haven't killed him and hidden the body in the meantime."

It felt good to say, but Lena had no confidence it would work. Scott would be gone for months. Brian had plenty of time to dig in at the farm. And she wouldn't send anyone so unprepared out in the winter, no matter how much she wanted them gone.

CHAPTER TWELVE

It was cleaning day. Lena hated it, but if the farm wasn't kept spotless, any number of vermin or pests would take hold. And with so many strangers crowding them lately, who knew what was lurking in the corners and cupboards. They always completed it by the evening so everyone could go to bed after washing off the dust and grime in a bath.

The kids had surveyed the crawlspace in the afternoon when there was enough light. A mouse nest was all they found. The pipes under the house were in good shape, and there was no standing water to attract biting insects.

Then they worked upstairs, checking the closets for moths. And the adults emptied the cupboards and wiped them down with lavender oil. It smelled much better than moth balls.

Brian had managed to avoid doing any hard work. After pulling the tins of tea leaves out and pretending to check for mold, he'd put the kettle on and offered to make tea for everyone. Lena let him do it. She didn't have the energy to bicker.

"I don't understand why people would follow this Poorjohn guy," Mellow said. "He's not exactly taking care of his congregation."

"He's not leading a religion, it's a cult," Lena said.

"What's the difference?" Brian asked. "Maybe this guy did get a message from God."

"The difference is time," Ava answered the question. "If a cult can gain enough following and continue for enough time in the right conditions, it becomes a religion."

"But I don't get it," Mellow said. "No one is really responsible for the plagues. Even the antivaxxers. It mutated, right?"

"Yes, but people lost a lot," Lena said. "Grief changes you. And, if you surround yourself with other people who are stuck there, you have no one to lead you out." She hadn't thought this through before. Even so, it didn't give them the right to take the land from people who worked it. Sympathy didn't change the facts.

"I don't know," Mellow said. "We all lost people, right? I mean, maybe not family like me, but our whole lives changed. And we moved on."

"Just like a clique," Deb said. "At some point, people just want to belong no matter what it's like on the inside. A cult benefits from lots of members; a clique needs to be limited and exclusive. A small difference, but important."

"I guess that makes us the clique," Mellow said. "But no one wants to join us. They know how hard we work."

"Tea's ready." Brian pulled mugs toward him and started to pour. "Take a break."

"When we're done," Lena said. She took a mug of tea to the counter and continued to work, something she wouldn't have done if she was cleaning with toxic chemicals.

"You shouldn't judge Poorjohn," Brian said when everyone was focused on their chores. "He's like Lena, just trying to help people."

Lena stopped rubbing the oil on the shelf. Telling herself

to stay calm, she turned to answer him. *Like her? Poorjohn was a leech.*

"Not true," Keith said before she could speak. "I've met a few preachers like him. They were all over the TV in the old days. They really want power. They want money and adoration. Crooks, all of them. Lena saved our lives."

Brian kept his eyes on the contents of his mug. "I'm just saying, don't judge people because they made a different decision than you."

"I'll judge them all I want as long as they camp on our doorstep." Lena rubbed her eyes. She didn't mean to provoke Brian, but he knew exactly how to force a reaction from her.

"They don't have anywhere to go," Brian said. "If someone took them in hand with a plan for the future, they'd be fine. They aren't freeloaders, just people who can't find a place in this world."

"Yes, and they could use your skills to do that," Lena said.

She turned back to her task hearing Brian's chair scrape against the floor and then his heavy tread as he left them to go out the back door.

CHAPTER THIRTEEN

Sleep didn't refresh Lena like she hoped. A sense of urgency plucked at her mind with no concrete explanation. Everything needed her attention, and everything felt critical. She climbed out from the quilt as soon as the darkness faded. No one slept in on the farm, but rarely did anyone get up before dawn.

She pulled a sweater over her pajamas and peeked out the window. Her bedroom looked over the road and, lately, an encampment. Her throat went dry at what she saw. In the night, the missionary camp had doubled in size. It encroached on the road, and if she didn't stop them, they would control it.

She pulled on clothes, ran to the bathroom and then raced downstairs to confront the occupants. This couldn't continue. If she didn't act, the camp could be twice as large tomorrow. It was already too big for a few people to move along, no matter how many guns they had. Maybe she would ask for help from one of the allies now. Free passage between towns was critical for everyone.

She made it to the porch before caution slowed her. She

couldn't force anything. There weren't enough people on the farm to break up the camp. And if they could arrive silently, she had no way to stop more from coming. She didn't even have enough people to set a decent watch on the intruders. She leaned against the railing and tried to take a breath. Her hand was shaking, and her legs seemed ready to collapse.

The cool air and sound of the dawn chorus of birds helped to calm her. The camp was quiet. They didn't seem like a threat — if you ignored the fact that they shouldn't be there at all. She had time.

Travelers would come; the post would still move. She wasn't facing a siege, she was overreacting.

Food and tea and the company of her friends would help. And if not, preparing breakfast would give her time to think.

The hominess did the job. The small tasks of frying bacon and brewing tea allowed Lena's brain to work out a plan. She needed information to do that. Is that why she was so worked up? Because she didn't know enough to figure out the solution?

"I see we have more squatters," Keith said. He started slicing bread for toast. "It's not a good sign."

"It makes me long for the good old days of city refugees."

Keith chuckled. "You mean a couple of days ago, right?"

Mellow joined them and sliced apples. "I hope Pallavi can get through."

It was reassuring to hear her own worries coming from others. "I'll go down and find out what I can do after breakfast." She placed the bacon on a plate to drain and started cracking eggs into the pan. "Can you wake everyone up, please?"

Mellow went to the bottom of the stairs and yelled, "Breakfast is ready."

"I could have done that," Lena said, "but I guess it worked."

The kids ran down the stairs, thumping on each step; Deb and Brian close behind, both complaining about the noise. Maya and Mahir ignored them.

"Mom is on her way," Maya said as she grabbed cutlery and followed Mahir around the table, setting the places. "Did you notice the camp?"

Lena glanced at Maya. She sounded curious, but a trace of worry crossed her face.

"It's okay," Lena said. "They aren't bothering us."

When everyone was settled in, Lena told them her plan to head down to the camp. "Maybe they are just gathering and getting ready to move on."

Brian poured another mug of tea. "I can't imagine they see much need to hang out here. Unless they are planning to winter with us."

"That is not going to happen," Lena said. "We don't have enough supplies here to support them. And we aren't going to convert."

"You can't send them out into the winter," Mahir said. He moved closer to Brian.

Had Brian convinced the boy to take his side? She would mention it to Ava because Mahir needed a better mentor than her ex-husband.

"There's plenty of time for them to find a better place to camp," she said. "They won't be safe here in their tents when the weather turns."

"I guess we have time to build something for them," Mahir said.

"We don't," she said. "There are too many people in the camp. And we don't have the food for them."

Mahir shrugged and went to his seat.

"How can you be so sure?" Brian asked.

Was he just being provocative? "About them staying? Because we won't let it happen."

"No. Converting."

Lena pushed her empty plate away. "Good point," she said. "I thought I knew everyone, but maybe I'm wrong."

"You're not," Keith said.

"When are you going?" Brian asked.

"Now."

"I'll come along. It's not safe for you there."

Lena wiped her mouth to hide her grin. Did he think she couldn't take care of herself? Fighting with him on every point was just wasting energy. Maybe if he came, he'd show her how valuable he was, or he'd finally realize she could manage without him. "Fine. Get ready and meet me on the porch in ten."

When they approached the first tents, a child ran toward the center of the camp announcing their presence. Lena didn't understand how this camp could be so different from the world across the road. On the farm it was green and vibrant and comforting. Here, it was dusty and depressing. The contrast of the bright yellow flowers in the field surrounding them made the camp seem even worse.

"Looks like they expected us," Brian said.

Adults emerged from the tents to watch them pass. They were thin and tired looking. It took a moment for Lena to realize the people were forming a path for them by blocking any other options. Ahead, Lena recognized Faith, but not the two men who stood on either side of the woman.

"Let me do the talking," Brian said.

"No. I need to ask questions, and you are just here because you wanted to tag along." The words were harsher than she intended, but the atmosphere was creepy. Lena was poised to run, not talk.

"Fine."

"Welcome, Lena. And who is this?" Faith asked.

Brian stepped forward and held out his hand. "Brian Custordin, Lena's husband."

"My ex-husband," Lena said. "And your companions?"

"I'm sorry your marriage vows have broken." Faith inclined her head to the man at her right. "This is Fidelity, and this is Angel."

The two men nodded but didn't speak.

Lena ignored the marriage vow comment. "I see more of your congregation arrived last night."

"Yes, we have gathered many of the faithful."

"And is this it?" Lena asked, anticipating that Faith wouldn't volunteer information.

"I apologize for Lena's rudeness," Brian said. "Perhaps you can tell us what you are gathering for?"

Brian was going to regret that, Lena thought. His words were meant as a threat to her, but she couldn't be sure if it was about her retaliating for him interfering or another slight. It was like he couldn't hear her when she told him what she planned.

"Understandable curiosity," Faith said. "We are here doing Reverend Poorjohn's work."

Lena stepped forward, placing herself in front of Brian. "You are camping on our land. I need to understand what is going on."

"God's work." Faith smiled as though that answered Lena's question.

"In particular," Lena said. "Why are you here and not somewhere else?"

"This is where the Reverend asked us to be," Faith said. "The land is owned by God, not by you."

God didn't plow the fields. Lena heard Brian take a breath to speak. "And how long do you think you'll be staying?" she asked before he could say anything.

"Only the Reverend will know that."

"We'll see," Lena said. If they weren't interested in her point of view, there would be no more information. But what she'd seen told her enough. She turned to go, giving Brian a not so gentle shove toward the farm.

"Thank you for your time," he said before walking away.

While they'd been talking to Faith, a few more tents had encroached on the road. Lena couldn't tell if someone had moved or if more people had arrived. She stalked across and through the farm gate, then turned to tell Brian what she thought of his actions.

"Before you say anything," he said with his hands up in surrender, "you didn't get anywhere because you expected them to understand your point of view on your rights as a landowner. These people don't recognize your reasons or your authority and there are a lot more of them than us. You are going to need to change tactics."

"The first one that will change is you. I don't need that kind of help. You just make everything worse." She shook her head when he started to respond. "Look." She pointed to the road.

Two riders were stalled in front of the encroaching tents. Four of the missionaries stood across the road. The travelers said something to each other then turned around.

"They can't block the road, Brian."

"Well, yes, that might be going too far."

"Might be?" Lena turned and left Brian watching the road.

Next time it would be Keith and his weapons accompanying her. Right now, she needed to find a way to stop them creating a blockade.

CHAPTER FOURTEEN

"Is Brian coming back?" Keith asked, joining Lena on the porch.

Brian had only watched the camp for a few minutes before returning to the house to grab a gleaning bag and storm out the back door to pick through the remaining crops. Or, at least, pretend to do it.

"I guess we'll see him when he gets hungry," she said. Then, realizing she made him sound like a runaway toddler, she added, "I think he just needed quiet to figure out what his next steps are. Don't ask what he's planning; I've given up trying to figure it out."

"If he gets back here early enough, I'll take him out for a couple of hours to assess his fighting skills."

"Thanks." Lena nodded toward the camp. "What do you think we should do about that? They aren't like the refugees. At least they had a goal that took them off our hands eventually. I'm scared this new group will grow overnight into something too big to handle."

"Might already be," Keith said.

"I hope not. If we hadn't lost three people, I'd send riders to all our allies. If the towns band together, we can move them on. It's why we signed the alliance, after all. Maybe we can push these people to follow the refugees."

"That's mean enough to make Deb smile, and you know what she was like in school." Keith sat on one of the wooden rocking chairs. "Staring won't help."

Lena joined him. "I was thinking we should set a patrol up the road. Stop them drifting in without us knowing."

"One person can't do that," Keith said. "I guess a bit of notice would be good but won't stop them."

"Why do you think they've stopped here?"

Keith thought for a moment. Lena liked that he didn't just jump in with an answer.

"The larger places moved them on." Keith nodded his head as if approving his thoughts. "Maybe there's no plan. We aren't big enough to push them out. It might be they don't know about the alliances; maybe they think we can be overrun, and they can turn the whole farm into some kind of compound. Try to force anyone coming by to join the church."

"Who would have thought when we headed here that we'd be too small to defend, too vital to ignore." When Newton Cole started his war, he wanted to control the flow of traffic to the west. There were other routes, but this was the most northerly passage that didn't close for half the year because of weather. The southern ones were too far away for people in what used to be Eastern Canada and the Northeastern US to bother with. "I'm not giving in. The problem, I think, based on what I saw this morning, is that no one in the camp is allowed to make decisions. Poorjohn sent them here and he is the one we need to negotiate with. We need to find him."

"He might be on his way," Keith said. "That's what I would do. Send my followers until there were enough of them to quell resistance and then come myself."

"Good thing for us you aren't in the world domination racket."

"Not yet," Keith said, chuckling. "Maybe when we set up on our own land, I'll get itchy to take over."

"You won't get resistance from me," Lena said. "Most of the time being the leader is a pain in the ass."

"So, we have a couple of choices still," Keith said. "Find Poorjohn and make him send these idiots somewhere else or find some reinforcements and move them along ourselves — and hope they don't come back."

"Will you go to Crystal?" Lena asked. A rider could go that way without being noticed. Cross the fields behind the farm and come out on the road far enough away from the camp that they wouldn't be seen. It meant the missionaries wouldn't know she was even shorter on people than before. "I can wait for the post or other travelers to take messages the other way."

"If they can make it through," Keith said. "What about Brian? His training?"

"I can't have everything I want," Lena said. "Based on his behavior at the camp, he wouldn't fight anyway. So, we won't waste your time."

"Mellow or Ava could train him. Or you, if you could find the patience."

"To be honest, Keith, I don't hold a lot of faith that he would do the right thing even if he was the best trained fighter we had."

"Maybe he'll take to fishing. Most people can figure that out."

"I'll see if we can give him a few lessons," Lena said. "Not me. I'm not sure I should be around him with a gun or a knife."

"You might surprise yourself," Keith said, laughing. "Best I go tell Deb and leave now. I'll ride fast and be back as soon as I can."

"I'll get your horse ready and bring it around the back, so no one sees your equipment." Lena didn't really think the camp would attack if they thought Keith was gone, but she wasn't willing to take even a small risk.

Lena started pulling gleaning bags from storage. They'd be needed in the next few days or the birds would take all the last crops from the fields.

Keith had been gone almost a day. He'd be halfway to Crystal at worst; almost there if he didn't take a rest. The camp hadn't grown much overnight, so Lena's fears subsided into the background as she completed regular farm chores. Brian was still sulking, but his mood kept him from causing more problems. Or, perhaps, that was wishful thinking on her part.

"We have guests," Ava said, as she popped her head into the storage room.

"That's a nice way to put it," Lena said.

"No, actual ones. Pallavi and Evan are tending to their horses and will be here in a few."

Lena put the last sack on the mending pile and wiped her hands on her jeans. Two more people she could rely on. Evan was a nice surprise, but she should have expected Pallavi to come with an escort.

"Beer time, I think," she said. "And some snacks. Who's around?"

"Brian. Everyone else is out doing something." Ava pulled two growlers from the cold room. "Unfortunately, he was out front when they arrived, so we can't keep him out of it."

Lena tried not to react. It was nice that her best friend agreed with her about her ex-husband, but she couldn't allow their group to split into pro- and anti-Brian cliques. Although she couldn't think of anyone who would join the pro-Brian side.

"It's great to have another man around," Brian said as he led Evan and Pallavi into the kitchen. "Lena sent Keith off on an errand yesterday."

She'd asked the others to keep Brian in the dark about Keith's mission and now he knew. It felt like she was the one causing a rift; she was to blame for sides being taken. Maybe she was.

Evan laughed loud and long at that. "You think that leaves you defenseless? Believe me, I wouldn't want to face the women and children here if they didn't want me."

Pallavi hugged Lena and Ava before asking about Mahir. The boy was nowhere in sight.

"He's out with Mellow and Maya," Lena said. "He's healthy and happy, don't worry."

"I'm not." She turned to glance at Evan, then back to Lena. "We need to wash up. Can you spare a room for us?"

"Of course, we saved a room for you. Jason's is free," Ava said. "Will one of you take the couch?"

Pallavi blushed. "No."

Lena gave her another hug, happy she and Evan were together after the events that brought Pallavi and Mahir to the farm.

"Get presentable," she said. "We'll keep the beer cold."

Brian stayed behind as the two visitors ran upstairs. "She has come for the boy," he said.

"He's her brother, Brian. It's their decision where he goes."

"I thought those kinds of decisions were yours."

Don't start a fight. He's just baiting you.

Ava placed a platter of sausage, cheese, and apple slices on the table. "Maya will miss him."

Another problem to add to the list. They did need more kids around or Maya would need to foster somewhere. Ava would go too if that happened. Lena shook her head to bring her focus on the more immediate problem.

Evan came back into the kitchen. "Pallavi will be down in a minute."

"How was the trip?" Lena hoped the way was clear for people to travel.

"Not bad until we got near," Evan said, grabbing a piece of sausage. "Those people tried to bar us from passing about fifty yards from the gate."

"It is getting worse," Lena said. "They weren't doing that before, or not so close to us anyway."

"You'd be cautious about letting strangers through your home," Brian said.

"This is not their home," Lena said, trying to keep from raising her voice. "It's a road. They chose to camp on it. By confronting people, they are interfering with anyone who tries to travel."

"They didn't do anything when we kept riding, but I'm not sure how long that will last," Evan said. "If the camp grows... Well, I don't need to say it will be a problem."

"How long have they been here?" Pallavi asked, joining them.

"A couple of days," Lena answered. She poured glasses of beer and sat. "Only a few at first. They hid in the camp that just left. The city refugees."

"Poorjohn's followers, right?" Evan asked.

Lena nodded and told them how she'd tried to reason with them.

"We had to use force," Pallavi said. "Poorjohn was at Prosperity last week. But he only had maybe twenty people with him. We had guns and we showed him how far we outnumbered him. He gave us a sermon and left."

"Well, we don't outnumber them, and if you keep sending people off to spend time on the road, that will get worse," Brian said. "And they aren't causing problems as far as I can see."

"Blocking the road is a big problem," Lena said. "Keith will be gone for another three or four days. Can you stay until he comes back?"

"Sure," Evan said. "We kind of planned a visit anyway. And we brought guns."

"Shooting them is not an option," Brian said. He stood and loomed over Lena. "I will not put up with violence."

Lena looked at him. He thought she felt threatened by his behavior. She forced herself to be calm and direct. "What will you do if we decide to fight them?"

"I don't know, but I won't stand for it." He stepped away from the table and left the kitchen.

"Be careful," Evan said. "If they think they can use him against you, they will. They tried to drive wedges between people at Prosperity. And they were successful in a couple of cases."

Lena didn't know what she could do to control Brian, but maybe he'd calm down and agree with their logic.

CHAPTER FIFTEEN

Lena thought back to when the porch was a place to relax and think about the future. Now it served as an outlook on the growing camp. Evan stood beside her, sipping a glass of whiskey.

"How are they growing?" she asked him. "I mean, we should hear people come, right? It's like they are growing from the inside."

"It's a tactic," Evan said. "If you can't see the flow of people, you can't stop them."

"I guess Poorjohn has learned something from being turned away." How many followers could he gather? Maybe she needed to be patient, save the resources until the whole problem was clear.

"And maybe he's found some followers with skills in stealth logistics." Evan leaned forward as if to catch more detail. "I know how I would do it."

"How?" Brian asked, stepping through the door to join them. "It would be nice to understand how our neighbors plan to take us."

"Oh, for Christ's sake, Brian. None of our neighbors are a

threat. If you are talking about the people here, they aren't neighbors." Lena wished she could ignore him, but Evan needed to know she didn't agree with Brian's outlook.

"What are their shelters like?" Evan asked, seemingly unaffected by Brian.

"Tents," Lena said, "most of them barely more than a sheet and a few poles."

"Anything bigger?"

Lena closed her eyes to bring up the image of the camp during the confrontation. "No, but there were a few stacks of cloth and poles. What should we be looking for?"

"It doesn't—"

"Brian, let him answer," Lena said.

Brian glared back at her but didn't speak.

"I'd bring in extra bits with each group." Evan pointed to the camp on the road. "They might be situated to stop anyone noticing the activity in the bigger section. If so, they'll clear off soon."

"You think those people are capable of carrying more than the basics they need to survive?" Brian asked. "You didn't see them. They are on the brink of collapse."

"Yeah, I'd make sure to hide behind the weakest people. Puts you off your guard."

Lena listened, hoping that someone would come up with an idea to fix it. Evan and Brian could hash it out. She had all she needed to imagine the worst. No one would notice a few travelers walking by. If the camp already contained the makings of tents, the newcomers would seem harmless.

"I think they are preparing for Poorjohn," Evan said. "After being pushed on from the bigger places, I would be looking to gather everyone, be as strong as I can. Redstone is the biggest and best defended community around here. If they couldn't move this group farther along than this, imagine how hard it will be if the whole congregation arrives."

"Why here?" Lena asked.

"Because this is a good rally point," Evan said. "You are too small to push them on. I don't know if they have plans for the farm, but it might simply be a place to consolidate before moving on to Crystal and the west."

Brian shifted and seemed to be thinking up an answer to Evan's points. Lena wondered what it was about Poorjohn's group that made him defend them. Perhaps just another way to annoy her?

"They need to go soon," she said. "Like I told the city refugees, there's not much time to settle before winter."

"You can't send them out to die," Brian said.

Lena turned to him. "I didn't tell them to camp here, Brian. They won't listen to me. If they aren't gone by the time the weather starts to turn, we'll be forced to feed them. We don't have enough supplies for that. So, they will die, and so will we."

Evan stood. "I think I should check on Mahir."

Lena appreciated Evan for slipping away now that a fight was inevitable.

"So, you'll let them leave if the weather turns?" He seemed almost eager to believe she'd send people to die.

"No. I am going to do everything I can to move them on fast, so we don't all die of starvation."

"And if you can't?"

What the fuck is wrong with him? Lena clenched her fists trying to keep herself from stalking off. "Brian, if you started to help move them instead of constantly bickering with me, I'm sure it won't come to violence. You keep getting in the way. Why?"

He stepped back. "I care about them."

"So do I. Look, you don't really do a lot around here, Brian. Because of that, I'm going to assume that you don't get how little leeway we have without supplies."

"I pull my weight." He looked puzzled that she would consider him a burden.

"No, you don't, but you could start doing it. Maybe by figuring out how long our food stores will last if we start feeding a couple of hundred new mouths."

"There aren't even a hundred in the camp," he said, pointing toward the tents.

"Yeah, and yesterday there weren't more than twenty."

He glared at her for a moment and then turned to walk into the house. Lena hoped he'd take her advice and start contributing. If not, there was a camp of fanatics he could deal with. Maybe he could annoy them into leaving.

CHAPTER SIXTEEN

The next morning, Lena was still struggling to put a plan in place that wouldn't result in a fight. She remained convinced there was a way to negotiate a path out.

The gleaning bags had been mended and cleaned. Today, the whole family was going to gather the last crops from the fields — even Brian, if she needed to stand beside him all day. If she ended up having to feed the horde on her doorstep, she needed to be in control of the supplies.

"We should start with the garden," Maya said. "If Mahir and I go together, we can strip everything off the blackberries and other stuff. I can start drying them before lunch."

"Take baskets," Ava said. "Berries will turn to juice in the bags."

"I want to go with Mellow," Mahir said.

Pallavi handed him a bag. "You should go with Maya."

He grabbed the bag. "Why? I want to go to the big fields."

"But Maya is your friend," Pallavi said.

Lena realized no one had told Pallavi about Mahir's determination to stay at the farm. Now was not the time when he was in full rebel mode.

"Well, I can play with her anytime. I'm not going anywhere."

Pallavi handed him another bag. "If you are going with Mellow, you'll need more bags."

Smart girl. Maybe she'll get the boy to do as she wants.

The bustle of preparing to go out almost drowned out the knock on the front door. "Did anyone else hear that?" Lena asked.

Everyone stopped for a moment, and then it came again.

"I'll get it," Maya said, slipping through the open door and racing to find out who was disturbing them.

Too soon for Keith to be back, but maybe a traveler was stopping by. She could hope for a few seconds because a traveler meant a chance to send a message.

Not a traveler; Maya led a tall, stooped man into the kitchen. His body might once have been muscled, but now he was shriveled and carried the same about-to-die-of-starvation-and-weariness look as the rest of the people in the camp.

"This is Elijah Poorjohn," Maya said. "He wants to have a word with mom and Lena."

Lena flicked a glance at Ava, who nodded and then sent the kids to the garden. Having them in the house would make things complicated.

Lena checked where Brian was. He'd taken a bag about ten minutes ago, and she didn't trust him to stay away. But, for now, she didn't want to spend the energy needed to guard against his interference.

"I'm Lena," she said. "What do you want to talk about?"

He smiled, and although it carried the same worn out image as the rest of him, she could tell it had once warmed people. "I understand we've been inconveniencing you."

He made it sound like it was her problem, not theirs. Lena decided to play the gracious host. After all, it would be careless to waste her first time to confront the man. She'd been hoping for someone to negotiate with, and here was the leader. Best to start out optimistic.

"Why don't we talk in the living room?" she asked. "Perhaps someone can bring us tea."

"Thank you. Refreshments would be welcome."

Lena led him to the living room, Ava on her heels. She heard Mellow getting tea ready and reminding the others to hurry out to the fields.

Ava sat on the couch, leaving room for Lena and gesturing Poorjohn to the soft easy chair opposite. Had she done it on purpose to put him at a disadvantage? He looked uncomfortable with his butt low to the ground. They may have to help him out of it.

While they waited for the tea, Lena asked, "Is this the whole of your following?" It would be nice to know if she could see the whole problem.

"Most of them. But they are not my followers. We all follow God's path. I am merely the one chosen to direct us on God's path."

"Where does your path lead next?" Ava asked.

"God has not yet spoken."

Stay optimistic. Lena wondered if she was the only one who believed they would find a common ground where they would be able to talk without either feeling threatened.

Mellow placed tea and a few cookies on the table and said she'd be out with the others. Alone now, and unlikely to be interrupted, it was time to get to the real topic.

"What have you been told about us?" Lena asked. She was sure his followers lied to him, but it felt right to start with common understandings.

"That you visited us. That you are concerned that we are blocking the road, that you are an unbeliever."

"Those are the facts," she said. "They miss the heart of

the situation. This is our land. We fought to protect it. We made it fruitful, but not enough to support many people."

"I understand your reasons." Poorjohn sipped his tea and then struggled to reach for a cookie. "But those reasons do not mean we will ignore God for your convenience."

"Are you looking to grow your flock?" Ava asked. "There are few of us here. Wouldn't you be better looking for a larger community?"

"They resisted our efforts. But we have more instructions from God than to gather followers."

"A group of people looking for a home left not long ago. Perhaps your God meant for you to follow them." Lena tried to speak on Poorjohn's level.

"If so, he will tell me."

The sound of thudding footsteps preceded Mahir's appearance in the room.

"Pallavi says I have to go with her to Prosperity," he shouted as he entered the living room. "Oh. Sorry."

Lena stood to hustle him out with a few assurances, but Poorjohn spoke first.

"It is a godless place," he said. "It would make me sad to think you are forced to go live in that community."

CHAPTER SEVENTEEN

Mahir's shoulders stiffened under Lena's hands.

"My sister lives in Prosperity. And she is a good person."

"I am sure she is. Perhaps you can convince her to stay with you, here." Poorjohn used the arms of the chair to lever his body to stand.

Mahir looked up at Lena. "Could she? That would be great."

Why did it have to be Poorjohn's idea? "She's always welcome here," Lena said. "Perhaps you should get back to helping Maya?"

"Oh, she's just getting the stuff ready to dry. There wasn't much left in the garden."

Lena swallowed a sudden rush of fear. Had the missionaries already taken the last of the food they'd grown?

"Where did you go?" Maya's voice came from the background. She sounded frustrated. Mahir was easily distracted and that made him difficult to deal with.

"We're in the living room," Ava called out.

Maya came in, dusty and sweaty from the work. "Oh, you're still here?"

"I was coming back," Mahir said.

"I know. I meant Mr. Poorjohn."

Any other time, Lena would have said something about Maya's rudeness. But today, it might get him to leave. Then she could find out what the state of the garden really was.

"That's rude, Maya." Mahir sounded genuinely shocked. "Mr. Poorjohn is a guest."

Maya rolled her eyes. "No, he's not. Why are you being like this?"

"Like what?" Mahir asked.

"Like you don't want to be my friend anymore?" Maya's eyes blazed with anger.

"I might not be here much longer," Mahir announced. "You should be nice to me."

"I think we're done here," Lena said, hoping to head off a fight. "We need to get on with our day."

"I understand you are reluctant to accept that we have a higher purpose. God has called us to stand against the evils of these days." He didn't look at Lena, but at Maya. As though her behavior was somehow immoral. "I would be happy to share our teachings with anyone here."

"I'll let people know," Lena said, fully confident that no one would be interested. "But I think it's time for you to go."

"Perhaps the children?" He seemed unaware she had spoken. "No one is too young to learn the true path."

Ava took a step toward her daughter. "I think you should leave now. These children have chores. And we are too busy to sit around discussing moral choices."

"If the children wish to learn, would you deny them the light of God?"

"They don't wish to learn what you are teaching," Ava said. "If you don't get out of this house, I'll use my rifle to show you a different light."

Lena placed a hand on Mahir's shoulder to stop him

moving closer to the preacher. "I asked you nicely, Mr. Poor-john. Please, just leave now."

Even he couldn't ignore the tension. Ava's reaction might have seemed over the top to him, but the last time a stranger took Maya, it led to death and a lot of blood.

"Very well. I'll go. The children's classes start this evening around six if you still keep time. Ask anyone in the community. They will point the way."

He strode out of the house before Lena could say anything more.

"I'm going," Mahir said. "I want to hear what he has to say."

"Why are you interested?" Ava asked.

"Yeah, Mahir. Didn't you see how gross that camp was?" Maya wiped her face and turned to the kitchen. "Come on, we have more gleaning to do."

"Wait," Lena said. "I want Mahir's answer." If Poorjohn's message resonated with Mahir, how would they keep the child from making a mistake? Or running there to avoid his sister.

"He didn't tell me I had to go to Prosperity. He said Pallavi can live here. No one else cares that she's taking me away."

"We care," Ava said.

"Yeah, sure." Mahir tugged at Maya's arm. "If we're getting back to work, we should go."

"In a minute," Lena said. "Is the garden completely cleaned out?"

Maya nodded. "I think a bunch of deer got in there. Everything was nibbled down."

"Maybe join Mellow until lunch," Lena said, letting them go.

"You thought the missionaries gleaned?" Ava asked.

"Yes. And they will eventually."

"We'll figure out how to get them moving before it's too late."

Ava's assurance didn't settle Lena's worries.

"He's getting dug in," she said. "I thought maybe he would listen, but he's just like the ones who left. They ignore anything that goes against what they believe."

"I never thought we'd get to this," Ava said. "I almost understand what Abigail was trying to do for her community back then. I mean, we can't move them if they don't want to go. But we'll starve if they stay."

"I wonder if the small holders have ideas," Lena said. "If we all banded together, maybe we could deal with this."

"Maybe Keith knows where they all are," Ava said. She gathered the teacups and cookie plate. "When he gets back, he'll need to hunt, and most of them are located around the hunting grounds, so it wouldn't be a waste of time for him to reach out."

The smallholders had fought alongside the farm when Cole attacked. But when it was over, they slipped back into their homes. They were scattered in the hills and woods, keeping to themselves.

"I'd hoped he'd take Brian and teach him how to hunt and fight, but I'm afraid he'd be a liability if Keith needs to move fast."

"Brian did pick a bad time to stop sucking up to you," Ava said. "Forget about everything for a couple of hours. Keith isn't the only one who can hunt. We can go out tonight."

Hunting would force her to take a step back from her worries. It took quiet and patience to catch a wild creature. Lena didn't want to wait until the animals were out for that. "Let's go fishing now. While we're drying produce, we can do some protein too."

CHAPTER EIGHTEEN

By the time Lena and Ava returned from the river, lunch was almost over. Lena noticed a stack of gleaning bags sitting in the shade of the house. Not as many full ones as she expected. Had they been interrupted before they filled the bags?

"Is there any food left?" Ava asked as they entered the kitchen and dropped their catch into the sink.

"I put some sandwiches in the cold room for you," Deb said. She walked to the sink. "You didn't clean these?"

"Bears," Lena said. "I think we're training them to find guts where we fish. We could use the fertilizer as well."

Deb lifted one of the fish by its tail. "I'll deal with this. I think I remember some instructions on making the fertilizer in one of the books. It's going to be smelly for a while."

Lena took the plate Ava offered. "Maybe it will repel our visitors."

"It sounds like biological warfare," Brian said. He was sitting back in his chair and sipping tea, oblivious to the work that needed to be done.

"I hope you are joking," Deb said.

"Of course I am," Brian said. "I haven't a clue what you would resort to, but I don't plan to go to war."

"Will we have to fight?" Mahir asked. "I know how."

Pallavi glared at Brian and then answered her brother. "Let's concentrate on bringing in all the produce left in the field."

"We'll join you in the fields when we're done," Ava said. "How much longer do you think we need to pick the leftovers?"

"The rest of today," Pallavi said. "Evan is still out. I took him a sandwich earlier. I think he's watching the camp."

"The harvest is less than I expected." Lena picked at her lunch, worry reducing her appetite despite the hard work. She was almost convinced that the lack of harvest was normal, but the fear kept coming back. "I know there are more deer and rabbits competing with us; you think it's that?"

Mellow stacked the dishes beside the sink. "Maybe, but does it matter? If it was the city people, they're gone. If it turns out to be Poorjohn's followers, are you going to take away food from people who look like they haven't eaten enough in months?"

A little happy that she wasn't the only one who suspected the crops were being stolen, Lena shook her head and forced herself to finish her meal. "We have enough to contribute our share to the alliance and get us through the winter. We can't spare any more. We need to find a way to guard the crops we have left. But I don't think I can take away anything they've stolen. There's no good outcome if they won't leave."

"I hear Maya and Mahir received an invitation to join the Bible study today," Brian said, looking at Lena like he was expecting her to blow up.

There was no question in Lena's mind. Brian was goading her.

"I want to go," Mahir said.

"I'll go with him," Maya said. "It's probably not safe for only one kid."

Lena held her tongue. She wasn't going to feed Brian's little plan. And they weren't her kids.

"I think Mahir is smart enough to take care of himself," Brian said. "But it's good for you kids to see there's more than one way to look at the world."

"You shouldn't go," Pallavi said to Mahir. "They're dangerous."

Mahir pushed his chair away from the table. "You are not my mom."

"I know that," Pallavi said. "But I'm your big sister and I need to look out for you."

"By taking me away from my friends?" He ran to the back door and pulled it open. "I'm not going to Prosperity and I am going to Bible school. And if I like what Mr. Poorjohn says, I might just join him." He turned and ran before anyone could say anything more.

Brian had a smile of satisfaction on his face. He either didn't notice how hurt Pallavi was by Mahir's outburst, or didn't care. Lena considered packing his belongings and tossing them to the camp. If he wanted to cause trouble, it would serve her better if he did it where she didn't have to deal with the repercussions.

"I guess he didn't think it through," Pallavi said. "If he joins Poorjohn, he'll leave everyone behind. If he doesn't figure it out soon, I'll tell him."

"I'll make sure he's okay," Maya said. "Don't worry. And if we're there, we might learn something helpful."

Things were slipping out of control if a thirteen-year-old was the best spy they had. "Be careful," Lena said. "I don't think these people are as weak as they present themselves."

Maya rolled her eyes.

So, the teenage years are starting. "Don't forget we know how to fight," she said. Lena caught her quick glance at Brian.

At least she wasn't the only person who noticed the problem, a pity she was too polite to say Brian couldn't defend the farm.

Maya headed back to the gleaning, and Mellow joined her. Deb took the fish outside to clean. The others slipped away, leaving Lena and Ava alone.

"Are you okay with this?" Lena asked. "Maya is just a kid."

"So was Jason," Ava said. "I've come to the conclusion that saying they can't do something only makes them more determined. Besides, she's right. Both of them can fight. I'll make sure at least Maya takes something to use as a weapon, just in case."

"I never thought I'd miss the city refugees. At least they didn't try to influence the kids."

"How do you know?" Brian asked. "The kids visited that camp every day, sometimes for hours."

Lena counted on the fact that Mahir had never threatened to join the city refuges.

Ava chuckled. "I think they are too smart for that. We need to figure out Poorjohn's agenda. If the kids can point us in the right direction, we'll have something to use to handle the problem."

Lena picked out a clean set of clothes for dinner. A hard day in the fields was a good way to gain some perspective and cleaning up after manual labor restored her. The people camping outside created a problem, but not the overwhelming one it felt like before.

As soon as she joined the others in the field, it was clear no one had beaten them to the last crops. No footprints, no damage. The wildlife had worked the edges, but nothing more. Instead of making her feel better, worries about crop failure replaced her worries about stealing. Another topic when they had time was figuring out if they did something wrong when they planted.

That didn't stop her from putting a padlock on the root cellar and checking for other ingresses, like Pallavi had used when she raided their stores. The food was safe. It would be ready for sharing with the other alliance settlements in a month per the agreement. She hoped the camp would be dispersed by then or they'd have trouble delivering it.

She pulled on her jeans and then an old tee-shirt. It would be good to sit and talk with just the adults tonight after the kids left for Bible school and spying. She promised herself to let go of the fear they would be converted.

A soft knock drew her attention back to the present. Before she could say anything, Brian stepped inside the room.

"We should talk," he said.

"Not here, Brian. This is my bedroom. Mine and Scott's."

"But I wanted a private word."

"You are not welcome in here. I am trying not to constantly fight with you in front of everyone. You're making it very difficult, but I won't let you drag it in here; this is my space. I don't want you in here."

"But..."

She jumped into the pause. "No buts, Brian. We are not married. You can pretend we are all you want. Just because there are no divorce papers or even courts any more, we are not a couple."

"But we were," he said. "I know you don't want to remember the good times, but we did have lot of them."

"A long time ago." She struggled with her resentment. Brian had no right to make her feel badly about the past. And she shouldn't be angry at herself for not wanting him, but her temper kept heating up, and his constant pushing was wearing her patience thin.

"I only want to make things better for you. If Scott loved you, he wouldn't have left."

It was not true, Lena knew. "Do you think someone leaving is a sign they don't love you and they don't want to be with you?"

"Yes. What else could it mean?"

"I left you." Lena hoped that would sink in. If Brian really believed his logic, then it should apply to her.

"That was different. You knew what was going to happen. You tried to convince me to come."

"I did. But you stayed and now here we are."

"Okay. I get it. We need to build things back to a good place."

"Enough, Brian. You need to believe me when I say there is no future for us. It has nothing to do with Scott leaving. You lost me when I left New Surrey without you. We are two different people now."

"Does that mean you'll let those people die of starvation?"

"They'll move on when they realize we can't feed them. I'm not the one holding them here."

Brian reached for her; she pulled away.

He let his hand drop. "I'm the same person you fell in love with."

"You think you are. But even if that's true, the world was different back then. Everyone changed to survive. We need to work to live now. We have to hunt, farm, and make alliances and despite all our efforts, we are forced to fight sometimes."

"I could do that."

"Then why don't you?" Lena let all her frustration out with the question. "You refuse to do any work, or you go missing when we need hands. You wouldn't go with the city people who had a place for you and your skills. You dodge training. You freeload on us and think you can tell me how to run the farm."

"Is that what you think? I'm lazy and a coward? That I haven't earned the right to voice an opinion?"

"You are actively undermining what we are trying to do — get rid of the people camped outside."

"I just—"

"I don't want to hear it, Brian. Get out of my bedroom and don't come back in here. I'm going to eat a meal I helped create. I was outside all day making sure we'd have enough food. Where were you?"

"Grunt work doesn't build a future."

"Oh, you spent time creating a strategic plan for the future? Give me strength. You were shirking again. I'm embarrassed that I was your wife. Get out."

The last words seemed to get through to Brian. He closed his mouth on something he was about to say and stepped back through the door not turning his back to her, as if she were the queen. Or a savage animal who would strike if he lost eye contact.

It took a few minutes for her to burn off the anger building in her heart. She wanted to go down to dinner calm and cheerful. The others didn't need to be involved in her problems with Brian. Maybe she wouldn't be all the way there, but at least the rage would be gone.

When she entered the dining room, Lena saw the table was set and she could hear people talking in the kitchen. Sound carried in the old house, but their voices had stayed low. Perhaps no one had heard.

Ava came into the room with a platter of vegetables. "We're almost done, have a seat."

"Where's Brian?" Lena wanted to be prepared for whatever he planned.

"He packed a meal and said he needed solitude."

The others started to file in, bringing food with them. If Brian wanted to spend the night in the barn, or in the woods, it didn't matter to her.

CHAPTER NINETEEN

Two hours later, Brian still wasn't back, and Lena worried despite her thoughts when he stormed off. She reminded herself that she didn't care. If he wanted to stay out, fine. He was an adult no matter how much he acted like a child. Really, running away from home? Lena hoped he would keep going.

Unfortunately, he wasn't the only one staying out. The kids were still with Poorjohn. Far too long to do a bit of spying.

Pallavi and Ava joined her on the porch. "We're going to bring them back," Ava said as though Lena had been part of a conversation leading up to a decision.

"I'm sure they're okay. Maybe they found friends." Lena hoped her words sounded more convincing to the two women than they did to her.

"Poorjohn needs to understand we will protect the kids," Pallavi said. "He's testing us to see where we'll draw a line."

Probably true.

"Wait. If you both go, and something is wrong, we'll waste time wondering how long to wait before you need rescuing." Lena reached for the rifle she'd brought out, then reconsidered. Going in with a weapon might escalate things too fast. "I'll go. It will be harder for Poorjohn to provoke a fight if it's only me."

"Then we rescue you?" Pallavi asked. "What's the difference?"

"He can't play on my maternal instincts," Lena said. "He sees me as the leader here even though I'm pretty sure he'd prefer to talk to Brian. That carries some weight."

"And the leader would be the first to come," Ava said. "Yeah. It makes some sense."

"It should only take a few minutes to get Maya and Mahir to come with me. If something goes wrong, you won't have to wait. Go for the guns, bring Evan. I'm not in the mood for subtlety right now. Ten minutes is all you wait."

Pallavi crossed her arms and stared at the camp. "I promised Dad I would look after Mahir. I left him here instead of taking him with me. I left him alone when I got taken. I'm not doing a good job looking after him. I should be the one to go."

"He's mad at you," Ava said. "Believe me, I've had my share of encounters with angry kids. You never know what they'll do to push you away. I hate that I have to stand back and let someone else rescue my daughter, but Lena's right; she should go."

Lena didn't speak. If Pallavi insisted on going, she'd let her. But the best situation was for her to stay. If Mahir balked, her presence would give Poorjohn an opening for a lecture about how families should behave.

With a sigh, Pallavi let her arms drop. "I'll go find Evan."

Ava touched Lena's arm. "Be careful."

Lena glanced one more time at the rifle and then walked toward the camp.

How did these people work so hard and so quietly? Lena passed through the outer ring of small tents now organized like a protective wall to the camp proper. There were three large tents set up; the smaller ones arranged in groupings around a central fire and clearing. As she got closer, she saw how dusty the canvas was, how much evidence of poorly executed repairs she could see. A number of them sagged because the ropes were too loose, proving Poorjohn's followers didn't know how to set up a camp properly. Everything about the place screamed rundown.

She stopped and considered. If Poorjohn was who she believed him to be, then one of the large tents would be his. Perhaps one was a meeting place, but the third? She didn't want to blunder around going into tents until she found the kids.

It was always possible Poorjohn had taken the poverty and humility role seriously and lived in one of the small tents. She doubted that; he didn't have the demeanor.

"You are looking for something." Not a question, a statement. The voice came from behind Lena. She turned to see Faith standing there.

"The children. I've come to take them home," she said, proud that her anger was absent from her tone.

"They are with the Reverend," Faith said, pointing her hand toward the first large tent. "Let me take you in."

Why an escort? Lena didn't ask. She fell into step behind Faith and followed her the short way to the door flap. Lena reached to lift it, but Faith stopped her with a gentle grasp on her hand.

"We respect the privacy of people's homes. We do not simply walk into your house." She slapped a hand on the tent as though knocking on a real door.

"You don't respect my home enough to ask permission to camp," Lena said.

"The land is God's to give permission or not. We honor the fact he has allowed you to build a home."

"Enter," Poorjohn's voice called out.

Faith held the door flap open. "I'll wait here."

Feeling like she was entering some kind of lair, Lena stepped inside. The space contained a partitioned section that might be his private quarters, but where she stood a group of chairs sat around a small wooden table. Like the way old kings used to meet their subjects in their bedrooms.

Maya and Mahir sat across the table from Poorjohn. Each had a small chapbook in front of them. No one had tied up or hurt either of the kids.

"It seems we have lost track of time," Poorjohn said. "I apologize that you needed to come looking."

"Well, that can't be changed. Come on kids, we need to get going."

Maya stood and looked down at Mahir. "Let's go."

"I'm staying here."

"Why aren't you coming? What's going on?"

"I want to learn more." The kid's body vibrated with tension. Lena had no idea what he thought he was going to learn here, but he couldn't stay. She didn't want to risk Poorjohn inviting the boy to move in when he was in this mood.

"Mahir, Pallavi is waiting for you." She caught Maya's eye but all she got was a shrug.

"Well, she isn't my mother, so she can wait."

Poorjohn stood and stepped to Mahir's side before Lena could react. "You are welcome to return, but for now you must obey your elders."

Mahir grabbed the chapbook. "Can I take this to read?"

Poorjohn nodded. "It is a gift."

She didn't want anything from this camp brought back to the house, but there was no way to say that without sounding petty. She'd find a way to read the booklet later and see if she could understand how his message drew people to follow this man.

Mahir stood and took Maya's hand. "I'll make sure we get back safely."

"Good," Lena said. "I'll be with you in a few minutes. I want to speak to the Reverend. Let your mom know I'm fine, Maya." If Poorjohn was in a cooperative mood, maybe she could negotiate their leaving. And maybe she would find out how he managed to get Mahir to do as he was asked. It wasn't faith, but she wouldn't believe it was the appeal of a life like this. But Mahir was young and not thinking long term.

Maya said goodbye and let Mahir lead her from the tent.

CHAPTER TWENTY

"Thank you for allowing them to come," Poorjohn said. "It is important for children to learn a moral compass early."

What's the act here? Lena wondered. For the kids he's reasonable, and as soon as they leave, he's judgmental and patronizing.

"I think we're doing a good job of raising them to be good contributors to the community."

Poorjohn gave a slow nod as though he was considering her words.

"Perhaps, but I worry about their future without God in their lives."

Lena held her first words back. Staying calm was the key to negotiating. If she snapped back at him, she made herself the bad guy. And she was on his turf, even if it shouldn't be his.

"I'm sure they'll decide for themselves," she finally said. "Can we talk about your purpose here?"

"To bring God's word?"

"No. I think you have some other reason for stopping

here. There are only a handful of people on the farm. It's a lot of effort to try to convert so few to your way of thinking."

He gestured to a chair, but Lena shook her head. "I won't be staying."

Poorjohn paused for a moment. Then he smiled. "I cannot answer questions you keep inside because I'm not able to read your motives."

"I have one motive. To clear the road and send you on your way so we can live in peace."

"I believe that you believe those words. But God has shown me there is something more. Yes, you are small, but I grew my following a handful of people at a time."

Don't argue; change the subject.

"You'll starve if you don't go soon. Your only option is to leave before winter locks you in. Even if you go south, you can't risk being here in a month, maybe not even in a week. Your followers can't travel that fast."

"God will provide."

"I didn't notice God working beside us in the fields." Lena regretted the words immediately. She'd allowed Poorjohn to bend the topic to his ideology.

"Perhaps if you understood what drove me to God, what drove most of the people who follow me, it will help. Please, sit for a few minutes."

Lena took the chair closest to the door flap. She was not going to be trapped inside this tent. "Fine, tell me."

"Before, when we lived life with technology and mingled with different people from different cultures, we lived in strife."

He paused as if expecting Lena to agree. She didn't speak.

"Then the plagues. People died of diseases we thought eliminated. I lost everyone I loved. I wandered the ruins of my town looking for reasons, my heart filled with rage against an unseen enemy. I allowed demons to control me. I yearned for death to take me too."

Again, a pause. Lena still chose not to respond. His story wasn't unique. Most people lost family and friends as the childhood diseases mutated and took so many.

"I eventually found shelter in a chapel. I entered cold and angry, and three days later I walked back out with a purpose. Anger gone. God had shown me the way to a new Eden. I was to gather everyone into my flock, and he would show the way."

"It's pretty Eden-like right now," Lena said. "We live off the land and there aren't any wars. At least none so big we've heard of it."

"If you think this is Eden, you have no idea what paradise is." Poorjohn looked sad. This wasn't an act. Whatever had happened in that chapel, he believed everything he said.

"So, you think if you convert us, we can convince our allies to follow you?"

"I am not that manipulative," Poorjohn said. "I simply do as God instructs me."

She was back where she started. It was like trying to hammer a nail into Jell-O. "I'll say goodnight." She stood and moved toward the tent flap before he could say anything more. She had no more time or energy for debate.

It was almost full dark now. Lena knew she would make it to the farm without problem; she'd done it often enough that there were no surprises. Unless Poorjohn had laid traps. *No. That's paranoia.*

What she didn't anticipate was the change in the camp. Instead of turning in for the night, people drifted toward the farthest large tent. It stood almost outside the camp, only two small tents nearby. And not all the people, only about ten or so couples now she had a chance to count.

Poorjohn was nowhere, so she slipped in with the end of

the line of people. He needn't know she'd snooped. Maybe, if she was lucky, she'd find something to use as leverage to move them all along.

Within a few minutes she stood outside the tent alone, no one to witness her actions or stop her. Lena slipped through the flap and stepped to the side. Her eyes adjusted to the dim light. But her nose told her the story before she saw it. This was a hospital tent. There were sick people, lots of them, laying on cots, slumped in chairs. Two people walked down the row, one handing out water, the other assigning places to the people Lena followed in. Patients groaned or heaved or cried quietly and hopelessly.

No one had seen her, and Lena was far away from the patients. She took the opportunity to leave before anyone noticed her presence. She had found Poorjohn's secret. He couldn't move on because he'd brought a disease to her doorstep.

"It's bad," Lena said as she finished recounting the events to the rest of the farm, only Mahir and Brian absent. "Maya, did you or Mahir see anything when you were in the camp? Did you touch anyone, or eat or drink anything?"

"No. I told Mahir not to because we didn't know how safe it was. Because the people didn't look clean or careful."

"Where is Mahir?" Lena glanced around.

"Bed," Pallavi said. "He started sulking, so we gave him a timeout."

"Make sure he hasn't slipped out to go back." Lena rubbed her face, trying to keep the real fear — that the plagues were back — from her mind. She had to think of a way to contain this.

Pallavi returned to the living room. "He's asleep. And in his pajamas. I checked to make sure it wasn't an act."

"He's determined to stick with us," Ava said. "He can, you know."

"Yes. We can't go anywhere now," Pallavi said. "Until this sickness is cured, or we prove it's not contagious, we're quarantined."

Another reason to get things under control.

"They took us to Poorjohn's tent pretty fast," Maya said. "I saw that woman who came to us first. She was talking to a couple of other people. They all looked better than everyone else. No, not better, I guess. Cleaner... less like a follower. I can't really explain it."

If Poorjohn's new Eden required the death of his followers, she had to find out. And if it did, no matter how much she didn't want to use force, she would drive them off.

"What was the Bible study like?" she asked. Surely there would be a clue in that.

"Mom told me some stuff to look for," Maya said. "In case it turned out weird; like they tried to sell us to someone or something."

"I'm not sure that happens much now that we are just small communities," Ava said. "Too hard to hide your activities from the neighbors. And no way to reach out to others like you."

"Anyway, he gave us stuff to read and talked about how God wanted everyone to be good to each other and live a life of service. I don't know what that means."

Deb leaned forward. "Before, there were people who only lived to make money and spend it on illegal or immoral things. I don't think anyone lives that way now."

"It doesn't sound dangerous though," Lena said. "We should keep alert for any signs of things like Heaven's Gate or Jonestown just in case. I'm sure they looked harmless until the bodies started to drop."

"Whatever he plans," Deb said, "we must help those sick

people. I need to see them so I can try to figure out what they are suffering from."

"We need to ask permission. There's too many of them for us to just go in," Lena said. "At least to start with. I don't understand how he can preach about God's love and then turn away help. Let's get some sleep and then I'll go out in the morning."

CHAPTER TWENTY-ONE

After the breakfast dishes were cleared, Deb put a medical book on the table and a box containing some of their medicinal herbs. Lena sat with her, going over a plan.

"What were the symptoms?" Deb asked. "If I can narrow it down before we ask for permission to help, we'll be more effective."

"I can guess at some," Lena said, "but there may be others I wouldn't notice."

"Yes, that's part of the problem these days — no scans or lab tests. If we ever get our hands on a blood pressure cuff and some stethoscopes, we'll be the leading medical center in the whole area. Without them, it's all guess, Lena. Tell me what you saw." She pulled a pencil and paper from her pocket.

"Vomiting was obvious by the smell and a few people were still struggling with it. I saw some plates of food sitting beside cots looking like they'd been left a while."

"So maybe loss of appetite." Deb made a note. "What else?"

"Coughing. Some people seemed unable to stop. A couple of the people I followed stumbled, like they were dizzy. I heard some gasping, but that might be because of a coughing fit."

"None of this is really narrowing it down. Any rashes?"

"No." Lena sighed. "So, different from the plagues."

"Let's hope it's not that. How about jaundice?"

"No, but I didn't get close and the light was dim."

"Is that it?"

Lena closed her eyes and tried to bring up the scene in the tent. "Sweating. I noticed people dripping with sweat. And rubbing their eyes."

"That might help," Deb said.

"I can't think of anything more. Except the people tending them didn't cover their mouths or avoid touching people. So maybe they know what it is?"

"Or they are stupidly careless." Deb opened the medical book. "Give me some time to figure this out. I'll need to go see for myself, if I can't find anything conclusive in our books. If I can't identify what it is, I should be able to figure out what it's not."

Lena left Deb flipping pages and headed to the back of the farmhouse. The others were working with the food stores, setting up preserving and drying processes. They'd be canning in a couple of days. When that started there would be no spare time to help at the camp. She had to get into that tent today.

Movement caught her eye across the fields. Two men were leading a horse across the cleared furrows. Keith was back, and it looked like Brian was with him. Maybe some good news was coming.

Brian went to his room after cleaning up. Lena couldn't believe he was still sulking. Another problem for later, but maybe Brian would agree to help them sneak into the sick tent. And if not, he was an adult and should deal with his own moods.

Keith sat at the table, avoiding disturbing the items laid out by his wife. Deb sat beside him, hand on his arm as though to hold him with her. It still amazed Lena that two such different people could be so in love.

"They aren't going to help," Keith said. "They don't think it's a big enough problem."

"If it gets any bigger then help will come too late," Lena said, then told him about the sick tent. "When this is over, I guess I'll need to talk to Crystal about what the alliance means. Maybe the others too."

"You could withhold the supplies," Deb said. "They aren't fulfilling the agreement."

Lena smiled. At least this was a problem she knew how to solve. "No. I'll go with the delivery and have the talk as they store it. Maybe they'll feel some shame. And we can set up a tax system based on their refusing to help. Crystal's role is just that. Prosperity manufactures things that makes life easy. Redstone brings horses and other stock to the exchange. Crystal just has a standing army."

"I don't know if that will work," Keith said. "It struck me as more about not pissing off the good reverend than avoiding their obligation. And now, with the sickness, it will be impossible to change their minds."

Lena made her way toward the camp again. She had a list of questions from Deb about the sickness to help her determine a remedy.

"Lena." Brian's voice stopped her at the farm gate.

She turned to see him hurrying after her. "I'm busy."

"I know. You are going to offer help, right?"

"If you want a voice in the decision, Brian, you need to be

there when we make it. I'm not running after you to get your permission or opinion." She considered walking away but didn't trust him to let her go quietly. Any dissent right now would give Poorjohn an opening to... she couldn't be sure what he'd do.

"No. I agree. Things have changed if there is illness. Now you can't just chase them out." He started walking toward the tents.

Lena gave up and walked beside him. "I can if they threaten our health, Brian. But I'm trying to get information for Deb. If you are coming, don't fight me; help me."

"I know you don't think so, but you need me. Poorjohn doesn't like you. He enjoys provoking you. Let me help."

Not sure she could trust him, but knowing he was right, Lena stayed beside Brian. "Just keep on message, okay? We want to help. We need to learn more about the sickness. We have some medicine, but not much."

"And if he refuses our help?"

"Why would he? If he says no, we'll drive them out and burn the field. It can go another season of fallow. I know that sounds harsh, but we can't let the farm become a mass grave because Poorjohn is too stubborn to admit he needs assistance."

"I'm not here to undermine you. Let me do what I do best."

Poorjohn wasn't in his tent. His followers wouldn't talk to her or Brian, but they didn't stop her search. She headed for the big structure of the hospital tent. If the reverend didn't stop her, she'd go in to get the symptoms confirmed, and any information the people nursing them would give.

Poorjohn was standing outside the hospital tent. Four more people staggered past him to enter.

"Stop," Poorjohn said to Lena. "I will not let you disturb these people. Let God tend to them."

Lena tensed. Brian placed his hand on her arm and stepped between them.

He looked over Poorjohn's shoulder. "We are concerned that this sickness will spread."

"It is a test from God. If you are righteous, you need have no fear."

"Your God has a long history of testing the righteous," Lena said.

"Please excuse her," Brian said, stepping closer to Poorjohn. "She is simply worried. We can help. No conditions, no tricks. "

Brian was shielding her and acting like she was a misbehaving wife. Lena felt her blood start to boil. Then, thankfully before she blew up, she realized he'd shifted Poorjohn to the side. If he held the man's attention, she had a clear path to the tent flap.

"I understand that your faith is strong," Brian said, moving to block the reverend's view even more, "but God gave us medicines to help ourselves."

"And they did not work in the plagues. This tells me God wants us to let our faith heal us. We don't need medicine. All we need is enough faith that it is God alone who can heal us."

Lena moved toward the tent. *Keep him talking, Brian.*

"It did eventually. We developed a vaccine and made it available." Brian's voice remained calm.

"It is up to God to decide who will live and who will die. Those who die are lucky to be taken into his arms now and end their suffering."

Lena was within inches of the flap.

"How many have passed?" Brian asked. "From this illness."

The conversation was slowing down. Lena took the final step and reached for the flap.

"Stop." Poorjohn shouted the word at Lena. They hadn't fooled him at all. "Leave this camp now."

Lena considered ignoring him but acting now would not get her the answers she needed.

"As you wish. I hope we can continue this discussion another time," Brain said. To his credit, he sounded disappointed that the ruse hadn't worked.

"Perhaps," Poorjohn said and then beckoned three of his followers to escort them out of the camp. "God walk beside you in your troubles."

As they crossed the road, Lena thanked Brian for trying to help her.

"I was trying to engage him in conversation so I could come across as his friend. Then you blew it." He marched away from her.

CHAPTER TWENTY-TWO

"Brian, running off won't solve this," Lena called after him. She couldn't let him control the situation by blaming her for everything.

She found herself surprised when he actually turned and came back. "We won't get anywhere as long as you keep treating me like a child. I wasn't running off."

I should have known he would turn anything I said against me.

"You aren't a child," she said. "But I don't see you working with me on this. You need to trust me and tell me what you plan. I thought you were making it easy for me to go into the sick tent."

"No, I was trying to keep you from starting a fight. Even if I tell you I'm helping, you don't listen."

"That's not fair," she said. "You do just what you want even when you've agreed to a plan."

He glanced over her shoulder. Lena turned, thinking there was a threat coming from behind. Nothing.

"I am trying to help," he said. "Everything I do is trying to help. It feels like everyone is sabotaging me."

"You're not hearing me, Brian." Lena took a breath to

clear out her frustration. It was as if he provoked her on purpose. "We need to work together. When you go off and do your own thing, you interfere with our plans."

"I'm trying, Lena. I want to get it right. I want you to trust me. I just can't seem to do anything right."

"There is no right way," she said. "We simply need to agree on one way."

He looked toward the farmhouse, sighed and then turned back to her. "Okay. If I do as you ask, is there any way you might change your mind about being with Scott?"

Tension forced Lena to clench her fists. "Is that the price?"

"Lena!"

"No, I'm serious. Are you saying your cooperation is contingent on me sleeping with you?"

"Now, you are overreacting. They are two different things. I will try to do as you ask. And as a different topic, I'm still in love with you and want you back."

Don't make things worse.

"I love Scott. That isn't going to change. If I'm not with him, it doesn't mean I will come back to you. Do you hear what I'm saying?"

His face hardened. "Yes."

"Good." She walked past him toward the fields, needing some time to shake off all the emotions she had to keep in check. Even if it was just the time it took to walk to the back door of the house.

When she entered the living room, every adult was sitting and waiting for the report, Brian included.

"He won't let us in the tent," Lena said. She couldn't see any point in saying anything else.

"So, what now?" Evan asked. "Keith and I have been doing some inventory and we can't afford to waste ammunition on pushing them out with warning shots. We need it for hunting."

"I don't think anyone wants to force them with weapons," Mellow said. "If there are that many sick people, they won't be able to travel anyway."

"If they won't let us help, do we just leave them to die?" Lena had come up with no other options. They'd die of the disease, or of starvation eventually. "He is unreasonable."

"I can keep trying," Brian said. "At least he was willing to participate in a conversation with me."

"That wasn't a conversation, Brian. There was no give and take. But I guess it can't make matters worse."

"Depending on the seriousness of the sickness, they may still be able to move on after a cure." Deb's nursing instincts were strong. Knowing the people in the camp needed her care and couldn't get it must be painful.

"Did you work out any ideas from the symptoms I saw? If we went with something to help, rather than just trying to gather information, we might be better off."

"I need more data," she said. "If I try to do anything with what I have so far, I could make things worse."

"I guess we need to think of a way to get people into the camp."

"There is nothing we can do right now," Brian said. "Let's split up until lunch. A couple of hours might give people time to think."

Lena had no better solution, so they agreed to break up and think. Maybe Maya or Mahir would have an idea the adults wouldn't.

Maybe Poorjohn would change his mind.

She was still trying to work out her next steps an hour later.

She was in the kitchen, making bread, a task that usually left her mind free to think.

What kept nagging at her was the fact that this was the second camp she'd had to deal with. It reinforced how small and defenseless they were, and how their position between the larger settlements made them important to those seeking power. And that fact could mean this wasn't the last time they would need to deal with the same problem. They needed more bodies to discourage settlements.

There were a few ways to fix that, and all of them came with a huge change to their way of life. Maybe she should do what Keith and Deb were planning. Run away to a smaller farm. Just her and Scott. And maybe Ava and the kids. It was an option, but not one she wanted to take because it was running away from, not dealing with, the problem. Maybe instead of a school they should be building a barracks and inviting fighters to train with them. And that made her feel like she was building a fort.

This time she wouldn't let things drift after the crisis. When Poorjohn left, her first priority was to make sure the agreement with the other settlements was more clearly laid out. Crystal should have sent at least a few of their people, and if they weren't willing to help then they didn't belong in the alliance.

Evan walked into the kitchen. He leaned his rifle against the wall and drew a glass of water. He smelled of warm air and horses.

"How's the food prep going?" she asked. Everyone who wasn't getting ready for winter by repairing something was working to safely store their produce.

"I don't know. I went on a patrol to check exactly what's going on." He sat at the table and stretched his legs. "I rode out far enough to see if we've got more visitors headed our way."

"And?"

"I don't think anyone will be arriving today. But I couldn't get much farther without supplies."

"Well, at least we have a small break," Lena said. She shaped the dough into a loaf and dropped it into a pan for rising. Seven loaves ready to bake in an hour and no ideas.

"Brian is wrong, you know."

The non sequitur caught her by surprise. She joined Evan at the table before asking, "About what in particular?"

"That we'll end this without violence. I mean, maybe there's a slim chance, but he thinks it's probable."

"Good to know I'm not the only one who thinks that." Lena tightened her ponytail. "If a peaceful end is possible, it's not up to us. I can't let Poorjohn run this. We must be in control or... I don't know, but the outcome will be bad."

"The main problem is we can't talk to his people," Evan said. "We have no idea if they are willing to go or are as crazy as the reverend. What I do know is they are sick, and they'll be scared. That doesn't often end in rational behavior."

"We're too few to fight," Lena said. It seemed like she'd been repeating the words over and over. But maybe most of it was in her head.

"Redstone might send help."

"And they might not," Lena said. "I can't afford to send anyone else out in case this erupts. And, until we can identify this sickness for sure, we should stick close. If it's contagious..."

"I don't think so. None of us are sick and you've been there a few times, even in the sick tent."

"True, but even if Redstone sends a small army, the journey is a minimum of four days. We could be overrun by then."

Evan drained his glass and stood. "It's early, but I'm going out to hunt. If we're locked in here, we'll need more than just vegetables." He picked up his gun and headed out.

It was too early in the day. Evan was probably going to come back without success. These days game only ventured close when they needed water. Freedom from the human predators seemed to give them courage to range farther.

No matter what happened to distract them, they needed to go on a hunt tonight. Although maybe Evan and Keith would be enough. They couldn't leave the house undefended.

CHAPTER TWENTY-THREE

Evan had managed to catch a few rabbits, not enough to bother turning to jerky, but plenty for a hearty dinner. He and Keith were preparing to spend the night on the hills, hoping to bag a deer or two. Brian had claimed an injury to avoid joining them and taken a plate to his room. No one knew how he'd managed to hurt himself, but no one asked for details. It seemed normal.

When plates were full and the chatter had died down, Lena asked if anyone had come up with an idea.

"We need an inside person," Mellow said. "The reason we're stuck without a plan is we don't have enough information. Poorjohn stonewalls us. Maybe on purpose or maybe he's just stuck inside his belief."

Pretty much what Evan had said that morning. "How are we going to get anyone inside? Or are you thinking we'll turn one of his followers?"

Deb finished eating and pushed her plate to the center of the table. "We can't change anyone's mind if we're kept outside the camp. We need to send a couple of people in, pretend we are starting to believe their message."

"I will go," Mahir said, looking up from his plate.

"We need someone grownup," Maya said. "Besides, he knows you don't believe what he says. You argued with him when we were at Bible study."

No one had mentioned that before.

"Thanks for offering, Mahir," Lena said. "Maya's right. He won't let you see anything. We need one of the adults for this mission."

He stared at her as if scanning her for lies. After a moment, he shrugged. "Fine."

"Do you think he'll buy it?" Lena wasn't sure anyone at the table was a good enough actor. She certainly wouldn't be accepted.

Deb cast her eyes down to her lap and let her shoulders slump. "I lost four children to the plagues. Will God show them to me in the new Eden?" Her voice was soft and tentative, not at all like herself.

"And me," Pallavi said. She took on a less humble pose, but it was earnest. "My mother, my father. I have no one to guide me."

If it wasn't so dire, Lena would be laughing. She looked around the table and saw glints of glee in the adult's eyes. "You rehearsed."

Pallavi sat up and smiled, back to her usual disposition. "We figured the plan out while we worked. Deb and I make the most sense to go. Deb can see the symptoms for herself, and I'll watch out for her. They've met Mahir. They know he needs guidance."

"I don't," Mahir shouted. Lena would be very happy when he grew out of the loud, confrontational phase. "It's too dangerous, you shouldn't go. You aren't a grown up."

Pallavi raised an eyebrow at him. "If I can't tell you what to do, you can't tell me."

"Fine. Do what you want. I have plans of my own to work

on." He returned to the food in front of him. Lena watched a little smile of satisfaction grow. If he thought he'd won, he still had a lesson to learn about keeping a poker face.

"So, when are you going?" Lena foresaw all kinds of problems, but without a better choice, she was willing to let them try.

"When it gets dark," Deb said. "Fewer people will be around. We should be able to settle in. If it gets really quiet, we can slip into the hospital tent."

"And get kicked out?" Lena shook her head. "Try to find out what the followers think. Leave the tent for last."

"Okay, but there's one more thing," Deb said. "We kept Brian out of it. He doesn't know anything about this plan."

Lena thought she knew the answer but asked anyway, "Why?"

Deb looked to Ava.

"He's up to something," Ava said. "We don't know what, but we thought it would be better to be safe."

No surprise, but Lena felt a pang of sadness for Brian. Even the children were trusted to do what was needed. He wasn't even trusted with knowledge. "Fine. I'll keep him distracted when you go."

The two women took flashlights when they left. Lena had checked in on Brian a few moments before. He was asleep. She'd taken his empty plate and asked Mahir to watch and warn them if Brian emerged.

"Be careful," she said quietly to the women. "If anything seems off, you come back no matter what."

"We will," Deb said. Then she pulled Lena into a hug. Maybe the first time she'd done that with anyone other than Keith. "When we left New Surrey, I was so angry with you. But Keith was right to keep me in the dark. If I'd known what was happening, I would have reported you. I've learned it's more fun to be on your side."

Lena gave her a squeeze and patted her back. "I'll miss you when you leave, Deb. You've grown on me."

Pallavi gave her a quick hug, then the two women walked toward the camp. As they went, Lena watched their bodies change from confident to something less as they slipped into character.

The door behind her opened and Mahir stuck his head out. "He's on his way down," he announced before he closed the door.

Lena stayed on the porch. It was still her place to wind down at the end of the day.

A few minutes passed before the door opened again and Brian stepped through, two glasses of whiskey in his hand. "Thought you might want this," he said, handing one to her.

"Thanks," Lena said. "It's weird they are so quiet. It's like they aren't there."

"They must have banked the fires," Brian said. "If you let them on the farm, they could spread out. Maybe the sickness would die out with a bit more space. And it wouldn't make them any more dangerous."

"You can't be sure. Maybe it will spread to us if they come closer."

"If any more show up, the camp will come closer no matter what we want." He leaned on the railing.

"They've got the whole field to fill, Brian. I don't think they want to force us to react by crowding us more."

"It just all feels inevitable," he said. "I know what I said before, but Poorjohn isn't listening to anyone. I was in the camp earlier; he has a council of elders."

"You go there?"

"I stay away from the sick, don't worry."

"What about this council of elders? Do you think we might make some headway with them?"

"Probably. They seem worried about what's going on, but Poorjohn doesn't listen to them. And they aren't going to push him. They like the power they get from being close to him."

"So not everyone in the camp is a blind follower?"

"No." Brian took a sip of his whiskey. "They listen to me, Lena. Not like here where I don't fit in because I'm not a farmer, or a hunter, or whatever is needed."

"You could try harder," Lena said. "You could have gone with the city people, but you stayed." Deb had been as bad as Brian to start with, but she had skills and eventually accepted her future was with the farm. And now she was part of the family.

"I'm going back in," he said, swatting at a moth.

She let him go. The bats would be out hunting soon, and she didn't need him freaking out again when they swooped past. She smiled at the memory of Brian trying to swat the creatures who simply wanted food.

Only a moment later, she saw a small shadow slipping past the barn. "Mahir," she called. The figure froze.

Lena headed toward him. "I know it's you."

He sighed and stamped his foot. "So what? You can't make me stop."

It wasn't bad behavior. He wanted to help. She touched his shoulder and stooped to look him in the eye. "You can help us more by staying away from the camp."

"They won't hurt me." He looked over at the tents. "They might hurt Pallavi."

Lena struggled for the right words. "Deb will take care of her. I don't want you getting sick."

"But it's okay for Deb and my sister to get sick?" There was real concern in his voice.

"If something goes wrong, they are going to leave. If you go, those people might not let you come back."

"I could fight them." He pulled a knife out of his pocket.

"You are very brave," Lena said. She didn't try to take the knife away. "I think it would be better if you got a good night's sleep and be ready when Pallavi and Deb come back."

Under her hands she could feel him tense and turn a little toward the camp. Then he relaxed and nodded. "Just so you know, if they aren't back in the morning, I'm going in to get them."

"If they aren't back by then, we'll all go with you."

Lena took his hand and walked back to the farmhouse.

CHAPTER TWENTY-FOUR

It was a surprisingly peaceful morning. With a plan underway, Lena felt like she could stop worrying about the future. Of course, Pallavi and Deb would come back with good news any minute. She'd even convinced Mahir to wait until after lunch to go to the camp.

Mellow and Ava worked in the barn preparing the two deer from last night's hunt for preserving. Lena sat working with Brian on inventorying the supplies and creating a scavenge list. Even he seemed to be happy to cooperate.

The door banged open and then slammed shut.

"I guess we shouldn't expect the quiet to last long," Lena said. She turned in her chair to see Deb and Pallavi cross to the kitchen, Mahir pulling his sister forward. "What happened?"

Deb's hair was in disarray and her face covered in dirt. Pallavi's shirt had a strip torn off at the hem and it looked like her lip was swelling.

"They kicked us out," Deb said. "It's okay, we're fine. But we didn't get to see the sick tent."

"I would have stopped them hurting you," Mahir

announced. "You can't go back there without me. I was right, it is too dangerous."

"We aren't hurt, Mahir," Pallavi said. "Not much anyway."

Pallavi filled two glasses from the sink and joined them at the table. Both women took long drinks before sitting back.

"I did see some people staggering to the tent," Deb said. "But when I tried to go in, one of Poorjohn's elders stopped us and took us to him. Like we were on trial."

"He didn't believe us," Pallavi said. "I'm sorry, Lena. Things kind of went downhill after he called us liars."

"Take a breath and just tell me," Lena said. *How bad can it be?*

Deb took two dishcloths and wet them under the tap. She handed one to Pallavi and both women wiped their faces.

"We'll need a bath," she said. "Telling the story won't take long. Are you sure you don't want everyone here?"

Brian closed the notebook they'd been working on. "It will take too long, and neither of you look like you can wait. Did you sleep at all?"

Lena braced for some kind of complaint from him, but he didn't say anything else. Was he finally seeing Poorjohn as a threat?

"When we arrived, they put us in a tent in the middle of the camp," Pallavi said. "It wasn't that far to the sick tent. So, we stayed up, hoping to slip inside when no one was around. But our plan didn't work. People came and went all night. There's definitely something wrong."

"We managed to get close at dawn," Deb said. "That's when they caught us. Poorjohn asked us why we'd come to the camp. We gave the cover story, but he didn't buy it. He started yelling we were spies and our interference was spreading the disease. He claimed it came from the farm."

"You should have seen him," Pallavi said. "He's crazy,

Lena. I thought he was going to order people to run us off, maybe beat us up."

"His advisers stopped things before he made a declaration of war," Deb said. "I don't think they believed him. Maybe because we aren't sick."

"I pointed that out," Pallavi said. "I mean, we had no reason to keep pretending."

"What did he say to that?" Lena had no intention of staying out of the camp. Partly because she was afraid the sickness wouldn't stay there, but mostly because she couldn't sit by and leave people to die if there was a chance she could prevent it.

"He just gave us a creepy smile and said we wouldn't poison ourselves." Pallavi looked to Deb.

"When we left, one of his followers asked why we weren't helping them. Our escort pulled us away and we struggled a bit." Deb pointed to the mess of hair and dirt. "But we didn't get a chance to answer. I think he's telling them we either caused the disease or we refuse to help."

"That gives us a way in," Brian said. "If we go in with supplies to help, people will see what he said isn't true. They will let you do what you need to."

"We can't count on them being that logical," Lena said. "They could be blinded by the ideology. The good thing is, if someone was willing to ask you, they aren't all just sheep."

"We need another plan," Deb said, yawning.

"Go clean up and have a nap," Lena said. "I need to give this some thought."

CHAPTER TWENTY-FIVE

The discussion wasn't going well. Lena had updated the entire group while their two spies slept. Now, everyone was arranged in the living room and only Brian and Keith were talking — or rather, arguing. They'd all agreed something needed to be done, but ideas were scarce.

"If we invite them onto the farm proper," Brian said, "we can spread them out more, keep the sick people isolated. Maybe that's all we need."

"And then we'll have them here permanently," Keith said. "The plan is to move them on. If we invite them in, we lose that possibility."

"Not necessarily," Brian said. "It's not like we've got much chance of moving them now."

Lena's hope that the argument would result in a new idea disappeared. "At least we can hold them there." She pointed across the road. "There, it's separate from us and they are responsible to deal with their mess. If we bring them across the road, we can make sure the road is open, yes, but then they become our responsibility. I am not agreeing to that."

"It wouldn't hurt to let them stay," Brian said, unwilling to let go of the belief in his plan. "More labor next year, more crops, more people to help defend us if we need it."

He had no idea how it worked. Lena gained a deeper realization about her ex-husband. He didn't understand how people needed to be aligned in their outlook. Everyone at the farm had different ideas, skills, and visions of the future, but they all believed in basically the same thing: you worked for what you needed, and you contributed to the community.

Brian still thought that some people should be different, and some work was more valuable than others...or, she thought, manual work was less valuable. He couldn't change. He didn't want to learn new skills. No matter how she tried to help him fit in, he would always be trouble. That would work in her favor right now. Brian was also easily influenced by flattery.

"Maybe we can't see a way out," she said, keeping her eyes on Brian and trusting the others to understand she was playing his game. "We've been fighting to survive for so long, maybe our ability to see the big picture is gone."

He smiled. Why hadn't she tried this tactic before? His ego was something she knew about from the day they met.

"I am a strategic thinker," he said.

"And you are very good at it. So why don't you go over there and try to find a workable solution. You know our position. They need to go. Use your political skills to make a deal with Poorjohn."

He looked at her sideways. She knew that expression. He wanted to believe her, but he couldn't squelch his suspicions.

"For a real negotiation, we need fall back positions," he said. "What can I give him?"

Now the others jumped in.

"Negotiate when they leave," Mellow said. "Maybe start with tomorrow and end with when the sickness is over."

"Be clear we will offer to help with the sickness," Deb said. "Don't negotiate that away."

Maya was whispering to Mahir. Then she put up her hand. "What about people who want to stay here for real?"

Lena had not considered that Poorjohn's followers would desert him. "We can't support many," she said.

"Only some," Mahir said. "And maybe they will have kids. If they do, I can train the new kids on farm chores. And maybe fighting."

"Let's see what happens," Pallavi said.

Lena let the conversation fade into the background of her thoughts. How many people would want to stay? Keith and Deb would leave a hole, but that left room for only two or three people. Until it got too cold, people could camp, but eventually they would need more than a tent. The same problem as before. They really needed to build some extra accommodation, but, once again, that would have to wait.

"We need to work that out," she said. "But it is not part of the deal. We can't let Poorjohn think we are poaching his people."

No one offered anything more. Brian looked around the room, pretending he was interested in their input. "So, my bottom line is we help with the sick people and the whole camp leaves before the end of September? That should give them time to find a place to winter. Like one of the old warehouses."

"We can give them some food," Lena said. "I'll figure out how much without shorting the alliance." Otherwise, she'd be sending them to starve.

"I still think it would be better if you let them spread out," Brian said. But his words held no heat. "If they are contagious, being crowded close together will make it worse."

"Whatever we do, we'll have a lot of bodies to deal with if

we can't cure this illness. And I don't get why this is so hard for you to understand. If we give them any reason to feel like we are welcoming them, they won't leave."

Lena noticed the kids slip out of the room and a few of the adults were getting ready to go. She didn't stop them; this was between Brian and her.

"Why does the solution need to be them leaving?" Brian smiled as though he'd suddenly had a brilliant idea. "Wouldn't the farm be better if we left it to a larger group who can work the land better? We all have skills to sell in other communities."

She was speechless for a second, shock knocking her breath out. Could he actually be telling her to abandon the place they had worked so hard to build here? To go on the road again? To betray the alliance?

"This is our home," she said finally, voice calm and firm. "Don't even think that is a negotiating point. We are not leaving. If you promise that, you'll be lying."

Before he could respond, Ava spoke, "Brian, my son needs us here when he gets back. Tik and Scott need us here. You can't expect us to hand over everything to people who just showed up on our doorstep. What's to stop anyone from taking what they want?"

"Don't exaggerate," Brian said. "It's just this group. We're not talking about everyone."

"It will be everyone," Ava said. "You weren't there when we came to the farm. If we hadn't been strong, we would have lost everything."

Ava was standing now. Lena waited for her to hit Brian, she seemed so furious about the memories their trip brought up.

"It was just a thought," he said, holding his hands up in surrender. "Fine. We have our plan. I'll go there. I'll fix this."

Ava looked like she was about to straighten him out, but Lena shook her head. Let him enjoy the small victory. If pretending he would save the day made him do what they asked, it would be enough.

It took Brian ten minutes to gather what he thought he might need. Mostly papers: his task wouldn't require him to stay with Poorjohn long enough for a change of clothes.

On the porch, Lena took the opportunity to make sure he wasn't taking a hidden agenda with him.

"Talk some sense into him, Brian," she said. "No matter what he thinks God wants, those sick people need help. Deb needs more information than I gave her, so we can find a way to help."

"That's why you don't make any headway with him," Brian said. "You are so sure you are right, but so is he. I let him think he's running the show. You should try that sometime."

He hasn't a clue that's exactly what I'm doing to him. "We can't let egos get in the way. Even if you can't make him move yet, his followers need to believe we are willing to help." Lena straightened Brian's shirt. "You know how to do this the best. I was wrong to try to push him into it."

"If they were on the farm, you'd have a better chance of talking to them."

Patience.

"They are not getting on this land," she said. "I don't know how to help you let the idea go, Brian. If they encroach through our gate, we will use force to stop it. Now, the priority is the sick people. If we are pushed, we will push back. Do you understand me?"

He huffed and shifted the bag with his notes from one shoulder to the other. "Yes."

"You won't offer it as a bargaining tactic. You will close it down if he brings it up."

"I won't let it reach the point where he can suggest it," Brian said. "Can I go?"

This was normally where she would chuckle and lighten the mood. Today, Lena didn't trust him not to take anything as permission to do as he wanted. "Good luck."

A lingering question dampened her hope for success. Had she just handled Brian correctly, or had she been handled?

CHAPTER TWENTY-SIX

Lena picked through the latest basket of potatoes. Some needed to be eaten in the next week or so, some would make great seeds for next year, and some would store well for three or four months, plenty of time to get through to the new crop. Brian had been gone for a few hours and part of her was surprised that he hadn't come running back immediately.

She tried to be optimistic, but the fact she had to practically twist his arm off to make him do something productive still irritated her. It wasn't just this task; it was everything. And he behaved like he deserved to be fed and sheltered anyway. There would never be a real place for him on the farm. The group was too small to need organizing and the work was too hard, and the weather too unpredictable for long term planning.

Was that why he wanted her to let the missionaries on the farm proper? A larger population would give him a purpose. A larger population would need his skills, make him feel valued; something he didn't feel right now. He didn't adapt well to change he didn't like. Probably the same with most people.

It wasn't something she could resolve, so Lena put the

thoughts aside. Brian was in his element with Poorjohn. He didn't want to go with the city people, but maybe he'd find a place with the current intruders. And if he couldn't, when she had the luxury of thinking time, maybe she would find a place for him in Redstone or Crystal. Prosperity was still too small to need an administrator, and perhaps still too bruised from the way Abigail acted in the early years.

Nothing I can do about it until Brian returns.

She put aside the thoughts and sorted a pile of potatoes to the side for Maya to experiment on. The girl was trying to dehydrate everything they produced.

"How long before we should start worrying?" Ava asked, handing Lena the box of pickling spices.

"It's been a day," Lena said. "I'll start to worry if he's not back tomorrow. The longer he stays, the more I think this will work."

She placed the pickle jars into the boiling water to sterilize.

"Because he is seeing more?"

"Or talking to Poorjohn. He wouldn't have stayed if he wasn't getting anywhere, right?"

Ava stirred the hot brine and didn't speak.

"You don't think so?" Lena asked. "I know that look. Just say whatever it is."

"He might have gone over to Poorjohn."

It wasn't impossible, but Lena was struggling to avoid thinking of Poorjohn and his followers as a kind of enemy. He was just an annoying inconvenience. But somehow Poorjohn always knew what to expect. She couldn't believe Brian was telling the reverend what she planned, but she couldn't quite dismiss it either. "What would he do if he has?"

"Tell Poorjohn to camp on the farm." Ava started dropping green beans into the clean jars.

"If Poorjohn wanted to move over here, he doesn't need Brian to push him. We couldn't stop it without a miracle." Lena grabbed the ladle and started covering the vegetables.

"You think he doesn't want to move in here?"

Lena thought about the question, realizing she'd been so focused on getting them to leave, she missed thinking about what Poorjohn really wanted.

"I don't have a clue. He hasn't asked for anything, which is frustrating. Maybe he doesn't know what he wants. Maybe he's just stuck in a role he no longer wants."

Ava pulled the jar lids and seals from the pan. "Believe me, there's something. In the absence of anything for sure, I'd bet he's looking for some kind of power. He is in charge there, they don't question him, and he likes it."

"Maybe Brian will tell us when he gets back." Lena topped off the last few jars and stepped back to let Ava work. This new question deserved some thought.

Evan and Keith were preparing the grill. Tonight, they were going to have a barbecue and ignore what was happening across the road.

In the kitchen, Deb was prepping the meat, and Lena making salad. This was what she loved the most about the farm, the little daily jobs of making a home.

She heard the front door close quietly and Brian stepped through the doorway a moment later. He looked exhausted.

"Stay there, please," Lena said. "Deb, can we make sure he's not sick?"

Deb stacked the last steak on the platter and washed her hands. "No. He is definitely sick. Brian, don't come in here. I'll come to you. Go sit on the couch."

Deb drew a jug of water from the cold room and took a glass to the living room, telling Lena not to come with her until she made sure it was safe.

Lena stood in the doorway watching Deb attend to Brian. She handed him a glass of water and started asking him questions in a low voice. She checked his temperature with the back of her hand and then beckoned Lena in.

"He didn't go into the sick tent. I can't think of how he became ill, but it wasn't through contact. The people working in the tent aren't getting sick either."

"Will we be safe?" Lena asked, watching Brian drink another glass of water. "I mean, we can't kick him out, but if we risk getting ill, we can't ignore it and Brian could spread it."

"He needs to go to his room. I'll be the only one who goes in there. You need to wash everything he's touched." She bent down to look in his eyes, then turned back to Lena. "You didn't get sick and you were in the tent a long time."

Cleaning the areas Brian touched wouldn't be hard. Fortunately, he had pushed everyone away enough that he had his own room. "Can you tell us anything?" she asked him.

It seemed to take an effort for him to speak. "I couldn't make a deal. He's not moving, and I have no idea what leverage we can find. He's adept at dodging all my questions and ignoring all my suggestions. He fed me and gave me a bed. That's it." He wiped his forehead on his sleeve. "I started feeling bad this morning; it's getting worse."

"Okay, get rest," she said. "Deb, I guess you have a test subject. I'll keep an eye on everyone else for symptoms."

"One more thing," Brian said. "Mahir was there playing with the camp kids."

She watched them head to Brian's room. To his credit, he kept his hands in his pockets and didn't touch anything else on his way. Mahir's actions were a problem, but he was healthy, so maybe kids were immune.

Lena filled a bucket with hot water and grabbed a bar of soap and two rags. Starting at the couch, she worked her way to the front porch and cleaned the stairs and railings. It was time to prepare for a fight even if they could still avoid one.

CHAPTER TWENTY-SEVEN

Deb spent most of the afternoon and evening with Brian. She'd taken food to him and told everyone to stay away. Lena finished inventorying the ammunition and talking about how best to use force to keep Poorjohn from invading the farm. That's what it felt like to her now. No longer willing to passively wait her out, he'd let Brian get sick and sent him home.

She stood outside his door and listened. Deb was talking but too quietly for her to catch the actual words. She knocked and stood back from the door.

Deb peered out and then joined Lena in the hall. "He's better. I've given him something to calm him down a little."

"And? Are we all going to catch this sickness?"

Deb shook her head. "Poison. He's not sick. As soon as he drank water and ate, he started to improve. Sickness doesn't respond that fast."

"Poorjohn poisoned him?" Lena couldn't quite grasp what Deb said. "Why?"

"What exactly did you see in the tent?"

Lena thought about her short visit to the sick tent.

"People were shaky and sweating. People had been sick, rubbing their eyes. I told you all this before."

"Brian says he was feeling nauseous, but not enough to vomit. He said his mouth was full of spit and his heart was racing."

The upside of him getting sick, Lena thought, we have more symptoms to look at. "What do you think we're dealing with?"

"I'll need to look," Deb said. "Brian mentioned that the food tasted kind of off, bitter but not so bad he couldn't eat it. I think maybe I can find the cause now. And hopefully we can make an antidote."

"Will Brian need the cure?" Lena didn't want him to die no matter how annoying he was.

"He'll probably be okay tomorrow, maybe need a bit more rest for a few days. If I can figure this out, and make an antidote, we could use it on the people in the camp."

"Of course we will. I guess if Poorjohn doesn't find a way to stop us," Lena said. "What do we need to do?"

"This is where I miss the Internet. I'm in for a night of reading. Let me get to the books. I've got a guess, but I want to check the symptoms and some of them are pretty common."

Lena watched Deb head downstairs to research. She glanced at Brian's door. Should she check on him? No. She didn't want to hear him complain and he needed rest. If he had permission to feel weak, he would stay in his room for a couple of days. It would be nice to have a break from the constant aggravation.

There was nothing Lena could do for Brian, but she could track down Mahir.

It didn't take long. She found him in the kitchen eating toast.

"How are you feeling?" she asked.

"I'm fine, why?"

He looked as healthy as he had the last time she'd seen him. "Where have you been?" Perhaps Brian was wrong.

Mahir looked out the window and chewed on his toast. "I did all my chores."

"I know. Where did you go after that?"

He turned back and Lena could see the fight in his stare. "I was at the camp, okay? There are kids there and we played tag. I don't have anyone here to play with."

Lena reminded herself that the boy was healthy, and he was right. Maya was a good friend, but too old for games like tag. "Are those kids feeling okay?"

"You mean are they sick too, and I might have brought it here?" Now he was angry. "I am not stupid. I stayed away from the sick tent. The kids are all okay and no one told me not to play with them."

He ran out the back door before Lena could say anything more.

Lena sat with Deb at the kitchen table, medical books on poison open and scratch pads in front of them.

"There's so many here," Lena said. "How will we figure it out?"

Deb ran her finger down the index. "We can rule out a couple of areas right away. No isotopes, we can't make that kind of poison and the symptoms don't get better, ever. We can actually do that with a lot of the rest; some poisons just kill you."

"Isn't there arsenic in the soil?"

"Not enough concentration to cause harm, and it takes a long time for the symptoms to show up, and they are different. But I think we are looking for some kind of botanical."

Almost every plant could be poisonous in the right

concentrations, Lena thought. "There are weeds that could work," she said.

"I haven't seen any of the worse ones, and mostly they leave a rash of some sort." Deb flipped to a section of the thickest book. "Here are the common plants that are poisonous naturally."

They worked their way down the list, eliminating every one of the plants.

"What could be made into a poison," Lena asked, "if someone used a plant that isn't a problem unless it's in food or drink?"

Deb flipped to another list. "Not that many in this area. Lily of the Valley? Just the water can be deadly." She looked up the reference in another book. "Nope, wrong symptoms and it's pretty potent."

This is going to take forever.

"What if we look at this the other way around?" Lena said. "What plants around us could be used?"

CHAPTER TWENTY-EIGHT

"He poisoned you," Lena said to Brian an hour later. "Nicotine overdose."

"And you think he poisoned all the others?" Brian still seemed to think Poorjohn didn't pose a threat. "He wouldn't do that."

"He did," Deb said. "Tell me in detail what happened when you ate with them."

"He invited me to break bread. I didn't want to, they don't have a lot, but he convinced me. Said hospitality was a fundamental premise of the teachings."

Teachings that change with his whim.

"Did everyone eat the same things?" Deb asked. "If we're right, there's a reason only some people are getting symptoms."

"Poorjohn only ate raw fruit and vegetables. He said he was doing penance for his wasted life. The others ate the same as me, but..."

"But what?" Lena asked. "Everything is important. If he's killing his followers, we need to stop him."

"Everything came on separate plates. I mean it was a stew.

But they didn't put a big pot on the table the just brought everyone separate bowls. I guess someone could have poisoned my food and only mine."

Deb looked at Lena. "He could just be dosing some people. Maybe randomly, maybe they pissed him off."

"What did the stew taste like?" Lena asked. "You said it was bitter, right?"

"Not really bitter. I remember thinking they don't know how to preserve meat properly." Brian rubbed his face. "I think I need a nap."

"In a minute. Do you think he's running one of those death cults?" Lena asked. "Are we going to wake up one morning to a pile of bodies?"

"I think he believes his own story well enough, but I don't think it's about dying," Brian said. "I didn't get that kind of vibe from him. But he definitely cares more about their souls than their bodies. Those people deserve better than that. Now leave me alone."

He rolled back on his bed and turned away.

She made Brian join the adults in the living room a couple of hours later. She was sympathetic to his need for rest, but they were on a deadline to stop this craziness. She knew it was too late to do anything tonight, but not too late to plan. The kids were in bed and that was probably a good thing. They didn't have time to keep Mahir from reacting to the news.

"It's a slow poison unless the dose is particularly high," Deb said. "Brian was lucky. One dose only needed a rest and some water to clear out. The others? Well they've been taking it for days. They will need an antidote, but we have some time."

"So, the question is, how do we administer the antidote to the people who need it without a fight?" Ava asked.

Lena looked around the group, hoping to see a glimmer of an idea on someone's face. Evan was leaning against the wall, waiting. Brian was just looking like it was too much effort to sit on the couch. Deb and Keith sat together, neither of them ready to speak. Pallavi, Mellow, and Ava turned to each other. That looked promising. She nodded to them to speak.

"We can't take too long," Ava said. "It's not just the speed of the poison we need to think about. If people die and then we come in with the cure, they'll blame us. Poorjohn will make sure that happens."

"He will make them blame us regardless," Pallavi said. "People like that never see themselves at fault."

"I know," Lena said. "I don't understand why people are willing to follow him even though people are sick and he's not doing anything to help them."

"He's their leader," Brian said. "If you do it gradually, people will believe anything. They stop looking for logic and consistency. He panders to their fears and promises a solution."

Finally, he's picked our side.

Lena waited for him to add a plan, or the beginning of one, anyway. He didn't.

"Like Abigail," Evan said. "We did some pretty awful things because she convinced us it was the only way."

"And she didn't go easily," Keith said. "I can't be sure what Poorjohn will do if we march in with guns. If he's willing to put people in jeopardy with poison, he might do something more drastic, like set fire to the camp."

"He wouldn't, would he?" Pallavi stood and started for the door. "We can't just sit here if you think that's a possibility."

Lena touched Pallavi's arm and nudged her back to the seat. "We don't know how he'll react. But going in with guns isn't likely to make this situation better. It is still a last resort."

"And how far are we toward that resort?" Mellow asked. "I'm not saying we should attack, but where is the line? When will we need to be ready to act?"

Lena was prepared to fight for the farm, but when she checked earlier, they didn't have enough ammunition to fight everyone. And Lena wasn't ready to make a list of the people to threaten, let alone shoot. She was still hoping it wouldn't come to that. What kind of a leader would rather let his people die than take help?

"How long before they'll be too sick to recover?" she asked Deb. "Let's not lose sight of the fact they must be able to travel."

"We can let them go in a couple of days," Deb said. "Some may never be strong again. But they have wagons to transport them."

"Brian, did you make any connections?"

"One, maybe," he said. "Faith. She came to the farm before. She seemed willing to listen to me."

It wasn't much, but if he could plant a seed with Faith, maybe she would sneak them into the tent to save the people.

"You want me to go back," Brian said. "That won't work if I go there. He has full control of the camp. If you want me to talk to her, she needs to come to us."

If she hadn't been there herself, Lena would think Brian was building up the danger to make himself look good when he faced it. But she had. No one talked to people in the camp without Poorjohn knowing. He had counselors spying for him and protecting him.

"Can we find out who he trusts? The elders, I guess."

"Maybe," Brian said. "You think we can turn one of them? Put them in Poorjohn's place? I'm not sure it will work."

"We can try." Lena looked around again. "Unless there are any better ideas?"

No one spoke.

CHAPTER TWENTY-NINE

"We can't do anything without the antidote," Deb said.

Another delay. But it gave them time to come up with some alternate plans, Lena thought.

"How long?" she asked. "And do you have everything you need?"

"I have enough of the herbs to make the treatment easier on the patient, but the antidote needs activated charcoal. I used the last of our scrounged supply on Brian. About eight hours before I make enough, unless someone knows about a stockpile of water filters we can use."

"Go ahead," Lena said. "Let us know if you need help. We can figure out the rest of it while you are busy."

"Be careful what you promise them, Lena," Deb said. "It takes a while to see results, and if you pick the wrong person, that could be a day, and they might still seem sick from the effects."

"I will. And you should be there anyway, maybe you can figure out who's likely to make the fastest and most spectacular recovery."

Deb laughed and then left the room.

"There's another way to make him act," Keith said. "Instead of looking like a bully and forcing him to comply, we could find a challenge. If we can make him think he'll win, I'm guessing he won't be able to resist."

Lena liked the idea. It saved them from escalating. If they did everything right, Poorjohn would be gone with all his followers. Unless he was the kind of man who reneged on his promises. And if so, that was a weapon they could use.

"What kind of challenge?" she asked.

Brian perked up. "To his ego, not his beliefs. He won't get on board if you challenge his teachings. But it's not simply the challenge that needs to entice him."

Everyone looked at him, just as Lena knew Brian meant them to. He was as bad as Poorjohn, only his weakness was a need for status, not power alone.

"There are only so many things we can offer," Lena said. "We've offered help to find a new home. We don't have money and it's not useful anyway."

Brian shrugged and waited.

He has an answer but wants to tell everyone why their ideas are wrong. Even when he is doing the right thing, he's an asshole.

"All the guy seems to want is for us to agree with his beliefs," Mellow said. "Would that be enough? We can lie, right?"

"It's not something you can prove," Brian said. "He'll need something concrete. Something other people will see as a victory."

"You mean we make the prize irresistible?" Pallavi said. "It might work, but..."

"What?" Lena asked.

"This is not my home," Pallavi said. "I can go back to Prosperity and take Mahir. I mean, you would be welcome, but I'm not sure you want to live there."

"Are you saying we should wager the farm?" Ava asked.

"It does give him what he needs," Lena said. "Will he see things the same way, Brian?"

"I can convince him to see it that way, but are you willing to risk your home?" He looked around. "I mean, the people who are staying. Keith and Deb are leaving, right? Pallavi and Evan don't belong here. So, that's you, me, Mellow, and Ava. Maybe Maya, I understand you've let her vote on decisions before."

She wanted to say he couldn't have a vote. Letting him do it seemed like permission for him to be back into her life. But he did live here. And three of the people who should vote were out exploring.

"Only the farm," she said. "Not the people, not the live-stock. We can go to one of our allies if things come to that. What do you think?"

Ava looked at her hands. She must be thinking about Jason and how he might return and find them gone. "The plan needs to be foolproof," she said. "But assuming it is, and the risk of losing the farm doesn't change, I'm in."

"Are you voting for Maya?" Mellow asked.

"We can confirm with her in the morning," Ava responded.

"What do you mean by the risk of losing the farm doesn't change?" Brian asked.

He doesn't live in reality, Lena thought. "It is already at risk," she said. "If we can't move them on, the missionaries will win simply by the fact they have more people than us."

"We need a challenge," Brian said. "And it needs to be something we can do."

Lena sighed. Brian hadn't figured it out. "The challenge is healing the sick. If we can do it and he can't, we win."

"And if he has the antidote?" Ava asked.

"He might not," Brian said. "He's not poisoning them

enough to kill them. But if he can, we just cure more of them."

"No." Lena saw too many loopholes in that plan. "You make him agree to give us a chance to show we can cure them. He doesn't get a chance. The challenge is all on us. Nothing to do with God or any other higher being. He picks people. We cure them in the time Deb suggests, and that's it."

CHAPTER THIRTY

Dust puffed under their feet as they crossed to the camp. It dried Lena's throat but was much better than mud. Now that she knew the source of the poison, Lena recognized the bright yellow plants, Nicotiana. Lena walked behind Keith, who led the way to the camp. Deb, behind her, had two jugs of the cure. She'd treated it with herbs to make it palatable after Brian said it tasted like dirt. Brian was already in the camp, doing what he needed to do to make the followers think rather than simply follow. She'd rehearsed their wording with Brian, but Lena was delivering the challenge, no one else.

When they arrived at the center of the camp — a cleared space where people came to cook and meet by the look of it — Brian joined them. It was quiet and eerie. People watched but didn't speak, no spark in their eyes, no curiosity, just patience, or possibly weariness.

Brian gave Lena a nod. Keith stood beside Deb, rifle cradled in his arm, protecting the antidote.

Faith walked toward them, and the little work being done stopped.

"Can I be of assistance?" Faith asked. "Are you come to join us?"

"I need to speak to the reverend," Lena said. "Can you bring him?"

Faith looked toward the tent, worry creasing her brow. "I can ask if he will meet with you, but he will probably wish to do so in private."

Not going to happen.

Lena reminded herself that these people believed Poorjohn. She couldn't just demand he join them. If Brian had done his job, Poorjohn would come out. If he'd screwed up, she would think of something. "I believe everyone will want to witness this," she said. "We have an offer to make."

Faith hesitated again. Not fear, Lena thought. At least not physical fear. Did she have doubts? Was it the fear that her doubts would be true? No. Wishful thinking. Stick to the plan.

"I will ask," Faith said and slipped away to enter Poorjohn's tent.

Brian leaned in. "He'll come. I need to go talk to the elders." He didn't wait for her to speak, simply faded into the growing crowd.

Moments later, Poorjohn joined them. Stooping to clear the flap, a smile on his lips and a satisfied gleam in his eyes. She had him. He thought no one knew. How he rationalized Brian's recovery to his followers remained a mystery. He thought he'd won before the contest started.

"You have an offer?" He glanced at Keith and Deb. "I see you brought reinforcements."

"Companions," Lena said. "We mean no harm. You can see we have only one weapon."

"Your ideas can be harmful. Please tell us what you have to offer and then leave us."

"You have sick people in the camp. We would like to cure

them," she said, ignoring his attitude. This was what they wanted. His arrogance would work in their favor.

"God will do so," Poorjohn said.

"Perhaps God sent us as messengers," she said.

The crowd inched closer. Keith and Deb didn't move.

"I doubt that, but you want something. Am I right?"

"If we are able to cure them, then we are doing God's work," she said. "I would like your agreement that if we are successful, you will pack up and go."

His smile grew. Good, he underestimated them. It was only a matter of playing the game until he agreed.

"You would withhold treatment if we don't agree?"

Lena scanned the crowd. They were listening closely.

"We offered help before and were refused the chance. We want to cure people, but you must give us permission, apparently. Our request that you leave when it's done is not the price."

"Why do you think you can heal them?" He didn't waver in his confidence that he had them.

"The symptoms," she said. "When I was in the tent, I saw how people reacted to what made them sick. We have medical books."

Lena stopped short of saying books on poisons. Her one job was not to antagonize Poorjohn or let him antagonize her.

"I will give my permission on two conditions. First, if you are unable to heal my followers, you will allow anyone who wishes to join us to do so. And you will accept us onto the land as long as God wants us here."

So, he was making it a challenge. Nice to know her instincts about the man were as strong as Brian's.

"Agreed," she said. "We need to go to the sick tent."

"How long must we wait for this miracle?" He smiled like a TV evangelist, all teeth and greed.

"Only a couple of hours," Deb said. "It is better if we choose only a few people. When they are better, we will treat everyone."

And we will tell everyone what made them sick if that's what it takes to get rid of Poorjohn.

The heat in the tent was oppressive. There were almost twice as many patients. The smell now a stew of vomit and sour sweat. Lena breathed shallowly through her nose.

Poorjohn didn't seem to notice. He rode high on his sureness that they would fail. He was different from the man she'd spoken to before. Then, he was calm and patient and nothing seemed to penetrate. Today smug, yes, but he was also excited.

"Deb, pick the people fast," she said. "Do we need to get them out of the tent?"

"If we can," Deb said. She turned to look at Poorjohn, disgusted. "How do you expect people to recover in this kind of atmosphere? Open up the side of the tent. Let in some fresh air."

"I was counseled to keep the ill separated from the healthy." He called over one of the attendants. "Do as she says."

He kept up a good facade. Only Lena's people knew he chose these people to poison, that it wasn't a contagion. And he had scapegoats ready at hand, people whose faith would be lacking, according to him. Lena wondered how he would find a way to explain himself when Deb healed the sick and told the truth to his followers.

"We need a small tent," Deb said. "I won't risk my patients becoming infected with anything lurking in these conditions. I thought cleanliness was Godliness. The least of your worries is dysentery."

"Do not lecture me." Poorjohn finally slipping the mask of

cooperation. "Choose your victims and move them to the tent across the clearing."

Lena could feel Keith fighting the urge to defend Deb, but she was capable of holding her own.

"I want clean water and blankets," she said. "I'll administer the medicine and wait with them. And wash the rest of these people at least."

She walked the aisles and chose patients in varying stages of illness as they'd planned. The antidote would work quickly on everyone, but the people who had taken the least poison would recover as fast as Brian. The rest wouldn't take much longer.

Mahir stood in their way as the sick left the tent. "My friends. You should pick one of them."

Deb looked at him and then at the crowd of children waiting for her to answer. "Are any of them sick?"

"No, but if it's a cure, then they should get it in case they are sick but don't know it."

Having Mahir in the camp would complicate everything. Lena joined Deb. "If they aren't sick, then we shouldn't use the antidote," she said. When he didn't move, she pointed to the people in the tent. "These people are very ill, Mahir. If we don't cure them, it will only get worse."

"But no one cares about my friends. Can I take them to the farm?"

Lena didn't get a chance to answer because Poorjohn cut in. "None of my followers will leave the camp."

Mahir turned to join his friends. They had disappeared into the crowd. Afraid of what Poorjohn would do?

"You need to go home," Lena said quietly enough that Poorjohn would not hear. "We will make sure your friends aren't hurt."

"Can they come live with us?"

She wanted to say yes, but this was not the time. "Let's get everyone healthy before we talk about that."

He glared at her and then turned to stomp away. His anger would fade, Lena thought. At least he's safe.

"You will all wait inside with those you are curing," Poorjohn said. "I do not wish you to wander around, possibly infecting my flock."

"Perfectly acceptable," Lena said. They would locate the source of Poorjohn's poison later. People getting well was the first step. They would be the proof it worked.

CHAPTER THIRTY-ONE

Deb spoke quietly to people on the cots Poorjohn had provided. The small tent was opened to the elements immediately after the patients were bathed. It gave the people in the camp a clear view of what was going on and allowed Deb to see into the larger tent that was now opened up.

Lena wiped the forehead of a woman who slept fitfully. She was one of the sicker people. Keith walked beside Deb as she checked the others.

It had been three hours. Poorjohn would be back soon to crow, but he would be disappointed. The water he'd sent to them wasn't clean. Deb had poured it out and sent Keith to the farm for more. Sabotaging their efforts was going to backfire.

Deb approached Lena and crouched beside the cot. "Two are ready to leave. The others are going to take a few more hours."

"Even this one?" Lena held the sickest woman's hand as she moaned.

"Probably by tomorrow. She should sleep soon. But he gave them so much, Lena. He tried to kill his own people."

"I think it was more of a miscalculation," Lena said. "Killing them doesn't serve his purpose."

"He's coming," Keith said. "The elders are with him. No Brian."

Lena patted the woman's hand and stood to face Poorjohn. It wasn't just him and his council. It looked like the entire camp followed. There were hundreds of people.

"It does not look like your cure worked." Poorjohn turned to the crowd. "It seems we found our home for now."

Lena beckoned the two patients who had recovered. They stood and walked to join the crowd. Two other patients sat up on their cots and waved.

"The others will be better by morning," Deb said. "I am going to the sick tent and treating the remaining patients." Keith followed her, carrying the two jugs.

"I'll get the rest of the cure sent from the farm," Lena said. Then, turning back to the crowd, she added, "We know what made them so ill."

"Come to my tent and tell the elders your thoughts," Poorjohn said. No thanks, no guilt. But did she imagine a tiny flicker of fear?

"I think your flock should hear," Lena said. "Are you afraid of what I'll say?"

His body tightened, and Lena saw the madness that drove him. "I have no fear of your lies."

"You've been poisoning your people," she said.

The crowd stood silently; Lena wished she'd brought more of her own people with her. The silence felt more threatening to her than any noise.

"That is ridiculous." Poorjohn stepped back.

"In the food. Not everyone's, but enough of your followers. Were you planning on creating a miracle somehow?"

"We all eat from the same pot," Poorjohn said.

The crowd thinned as people slipped away. Lena couldn't see if they were preparing to go or to fight.

"You don't eat from the same pot as everyone," she said. "You only eat food that cannot be poisoned. Raw food, vegetables."

"That proves nothing."

"You only poisoned some people. How did you choose?" Lena wouldn't let him disappear without justifying his actions.

"If people became ill, it was their faith that failed."

Lena looked to see how the remaining onlookers were reacting. A few were whispering conversations. Not everyone blindly obeyed. "So, people who questioned you?"

He slipped farther back toward his tent. Lena stepped toward him, all the anger she'd suppressed to reach this point bubbling up. "Answer me."

"It is their faith," he said again. "God is testing them."

"And your faith is strong?" She pressed him to answer before he slipped inside the privacy of his tent.

"Yes. My heart does not waver."

"Then eat the stew."

"You would have me break a vow with God?" He turned to plead with the crowd, which was thinning fast. "She is godless and strives to make us all so."

No one answered him, his followers waiting for him to prove the truth.

"It's nicotine poisoning. We can test the food. I'm sure you are still causing sickness."

"I will not stand for this. I order you all to leave now, or I will call down a punishment for your lies."

The crowd wasn't on her side yet, and Poorjohn could turn them any minute. She was standing alone; Keith and Deb were still administering the antidote, she hoped, but they were out of sight in the tent. Brian was still missing. This could turn against her any second.

"I told you to leave," Poorjohn said, his voice louder now.

"When the patients take all the antidote we brought with us," Lena said. There was more at the farm. What Deb had with her would help the worst cases begin recovery. "If it is not enough, we have more to bring. Or the sick can come to us."

Keith stepped to her side. "Deb has gone back to the farm. You need to come now."

The crowd was muttering. This was the moment when Brian should have done his part and convinced them the farm was doing the right thing, that Poorjohn didn't care about them.

"Now, Lena," Keith said.

"I will leave," she said to Poorjohn without showing the fear crawling in her gut. "We have started to heal the people in the tent. Anyone who needs it can come to the farm to get more of the cure."

"No one will come. They know God will save them."

She still had nothing to prove that Poorjohn was poisoning them, and he'd had a lot of time to brainwash his followers. Lena would need to accept this was only the first step in getting Poorjohn out of their lives.

"The offer is still there," she said. "I expect the camp to disburse in two days, regardless."

"You would send sick people on an uncertain road?" Poorjohn smiled now.

"You did that when you agreed to leave if we cured the sick."

"Lena, don't provoke a fight. You will lose," Keith whispered.

She didn't acknowledge him.

"I will seek council from God." Poorjohn wasn't answering

Lena but addressing the crowd. "We will leave if God says we must, not if this woman casts us out."

"In two days, the sickest of your people will be well enough to travel. That is, if they seek healing." Lena motioned for Keith to the lead the way.

The crowd parted to let them pass. Poorjohn was silent.

"Thank you," a woman murmured as Lena and Keith passed. "I'll send my husband to you."

A few more people mentioned sick loved ones.

At the edge of the camp, Lena turned to look. The crowd stared at them. "It's like one of those old horror movies," she said. "They are puppets with no minds of their own."

Keith took her elbow and moved toward the farm. "Not all of them. You made progress. I can go back to find Brian."

"No. Whatever he's up to, it isn't to help us."

CHAPTER THIRTY-TWO

Lena helped set up another canopy in the front yard. Their plan to accommodate the sick was almost complete. Unless Poorjohn went on another poisoning spree, they had enough space. Deb said she needed to shelter about twenty people for two days. The weather should stay good enough to let that happen under canvas roofs. Those who were only slightly ill would be able to go back to the camp to rest.

"Will they be able to travel?" she asked Deb.

"They will be weak, so likely not far or for long. They'll need food, clean water, and rest for a few weeks. Why?"

"I can't send people to die on the road. We'll make sure they understand to take it easy for the first week or two." She looked over at the camp. A few hours had passed since the demonstration, and no one had come to them. "You think we'll need to go back with weapons and force them to let us treat the sick?"

"I hope not," Deb said. "That's what Keith and Evan are doing, right? Checking on the reaction so we can figure out what to do."

The two men had left a few minutes after Lena returned.

They were intent on spying on the camp from a high point and then getting as close as they could without actually entering the camp. Probably not close enough to be effective.

"I wish Brian would come back," she said, then laughed. "Not what I expected to feel. Maybe I just wish we knew what he was doing."

"Maybe what we asked," Deb said. "I know, a faint hope, but we did ask him to help turn the camp away from Poorjohn's influence."

It would be the first time he did as agreed since he got here, Lena thought.

"Let's gather some blankets and towels. Anything else?"

"Barf bowls. Most of them will still be vomiting."

Keith appeared around the side of the farmhouse, leading both horses. When he got near, he said, "Evan's gathering the others. We'll report as soon as I settle the horses."

The sun was down by the time everyone settled in the living room. She noticed how small family groups formed. Pallavi, Evan, and Mahir together, with Mahir holding his sister's hand like he could hold her in place. Even Ava and Maya sat near each other. Was it a sign her farm family was breaking apart? Or had things always been this way and she was just ascribing meaning because of the threats? The warmth and company gave Lena a sense of peace, one she accepted even though she was sure the comfort was temporary. At least there must be news. If he'd found nothing, Keith would have said so right away.

"It's not much," Evan said. "We couldn't get close enough to confirm anything. He picked a good spot, hard to sneak up on."

"So, it's what we think from what we saw going on," Keith said. "Not sure if we're interpreting it right."

"Just tell us," Maya said. "Is it bad?"

Keith took a sip of whiskey. "Not bad, just... I guess we can't be certain."

Evan took over. "We saw a few people packing. Not a lot, but you got through to some. Maybe some of the others will follow. The camp doesn't all have to go as a unit, right? If they drift away, we still get them off the farm."

"It will take longer." Lena tried not to get excited about a little victory. "Any sign of people coming here?"

"The sick tent is closed up again. I didn't see anyone leaving to come here." Keith scanned the room. "We saw Brian."

What the hell was he doing to make Keith and Evan reluctant to tell them?

"In Maya's word, just tell us." Lena braced for betrayal.

Evan leaned forward, elbows on his knees. "He was talking to a small group — the elders, but also a handful of followers."

"It looked like they were listening," Keith added, "but we don't know what he was saying."

"And we all know him," Ava said. "He might be trying to form his own cult or sell them on a new Eden a hundred miles away."

Whatever he was doing, Brian would be looking for power or influence. He did nothing just for the benefit of the group.

Lena waited for someone else to chime in to defend him. She didn't want to be the only person always thinking of Brian as an asshole. No one did. They were all looking at her.

"I don't know. What you observed is exactly what we asked him to do. If it was you, Keith, or Evan, we wouldn't be doubting your actions. But Brian? He needs to come back and tell us what's going on. We can't afford to go in and drag him out without risking his plan."

"We need to decide what we believe he's doing," Mellow

said. "If we think he's helping, we leave him to it. If we truly think he's causing more problems, we need to stop him."

"If we decide he's causing problems, and we pull him out, only to learn he is helping, we screw everything up," Pallavi said. "The only choice is to believe he's helping until we have proof otherwise."

There was no real counterargument. Pallavi was right. If Brian was doing his worst, pulling him out wouldn't help.

"Is everyone okay with that plan?" Lena asked. No one objected.

"Next question," Deb said. "What if the sick people don't come?"

"We go find out why," Keith said. "It doesn't make sense that they wouldn't."

Mahir put up his hand. Lena recognized the not-so-subtle point that he was making; that he didn't belong, or she'd scared him. A tactic so old, she remembered doing it to her parents when they grounded her.

"Just ask," Pallavi said.

"Some of the kids want to come and live here," Mahir said.

Kids on the farm would be great. "What about their parents?"

"Maybe they don't have any," Mahir said. "Maybe they don't want to live with their parents anymore because they put them in danger with that guy."

"If your friends have no parents, they can come and stay. If they have a mom or a dad, they must go with them."

"Okay. I'll let them know," he said, jumping up from his chair.

"Not yet," Pallavi said. "Let's make sure what's happening with the sick people and if the camp is going to break up first. Okay?"

"Sure." Mahir slumped in his seat.

"Should we go find out why people aren't coming?" Mellow asked.

"We give them until morning," Lena said. "Someone will be up all night to accept people if they come. You all know what to do. Deb won't be on shift because she'll need her energy for tomorrow. I swear we will cure them regardless of what they want."

Ava stood and started gathering glasses. "I'll take the first shift with Maya. Everyone else sleep until you are woken for your watch."

CHAPTER THIRTY-THREE

The night passed with no patients. Lena watched the camp from the porch, but nothing stirred to give her a clue. If the sick tent wasn't so far, she'd sneak in to find out what was happening.

"The people we dosed yesterday need more," Deb said as she slipped through the door. "We can't let this happen, Lena."

"I know. I was just trying to figure out what to do. Any ideas?"

"If Brian came back and told us what was going on..."

"The longer he's there, the less I think he's helping," Lena said.

Deb sighed. Lena turned to see what was wrong.

Lines of exhaustion creased her face. It didn't matter that she could still be selfish and entitled occasionally, she was a nurse and knowing people needed her help and that she couldn't do anything was killing her.

"If we go in uninvited, we'll need weapons. Is anyone in that tent going to die soon?"

"Not from the poison, but from the effects, probably. I'm

most worried about dehydration because of the vomiting. They are weak and didn't start out all that healthy. Someone's heart will give out; another might have a massive stroke. And pretty soon, people's bodies just give out."

"And we are helpless, right?" Lena wanted to say she had a plan, but they'd done their best and she had nothing more to suggest.

Instead of answering, Deb placed her tea mug on the railing and moved down the steps.

Lena looked back at the camp. One woman was coming toward them. She didn't look sick, but maybe a messenger? Maybe they were being invited back to help?

As she approached, Lena recognized Faith. That was a good sign. Poorjohn would send a trusted follower to deliver the request. Lena walked over to join Deb in meeting the woman.

"I've come to visit my brother," Faith said. She looked around at the empty yard, taking in the canopied areas with bedding laid out. "Where are they?"

"Who?" Deb asked.

Lena let her take the lead while she observed Faith for indications she wasn't genuine.

"The sick. Most of them came here last night." Faith took a step toward the side of the house. "Are they in the back? Did you lie to us?"

"They didn't come," Deb said. "I'll show you anything you want to prove no one is here."

Faith rushed to the back of the house and then ran back. Lena watched as realization overcame her suspicions. She glanced at the barn and ran to the open door. That was the final proof. There was nowhere else big enough to hide the patients.

"What's happening over there?" Lena asked.

"Poorjohn is hiding in his tent. Some of the families want

him punished, but enough people still choose to believe his message that he's protected."

"If we come, will we be stopped?" Lena asked. "Will we be safe?"

"Yes. Come." Faith reached to pull Lena with her. She collapsed.

"Deb, get her inside and figure out what's wrong," Lena said. "We need to get to the camp as soon as you are ready. We can't let it end in a riot."

Faith struggled to sit when she was laid on the sofa. "I'm fine, just tired. We need to go."

"You are dehydrated and possibly starving," Deb said. "We have enough time to deal with one of those."

"No one has eaten since you told us about the poison."

They barely ate before, so they would all be on the brink of collapse pretty soon. Another reason they couldn't travel. Lena would not allow herself to lose hope of getting control again. "Do what Deb says," she ordered Faith. "We need a few minutes to get organized."

"We start at the sick tent, right?" Deb said. It sounded like an order, not a question.

"Yes. Deal with Faith. I'm not sending anyone to that camp to help until I've seen how dangerous it is."

"But they need help," Deb said.

"If we go in blind, we won't be able to help anyone," Lena said. "I'll let the others know what's going on. Then Faith and I will go to the camp. An hour, that's all, and it gives you time to prepare. There are a lot of sick people in that camp."

Deb trembled and Lena guessed she was desperate to fight back. If she did, Lena wondered if it would stop before someone died.

Faith wasn't the only one working on adrenaline.

"She's right," Faith said. "When I left, I would have said

you were safe, but I thought the sick came here. We need to find out where they are before you go in."

"One hour," Deb said. "Any later and I'm coming anyway."

Lena didn't bother answering. She hurried through to the yard where Mahir and Maya were working. "Gather everyone, please."

The kids ran to find the adults.

The herbal tea Faith drank acted rapidly, but she was still struggling to stand. Lena took her elbow and supported her as they crossed to the camp. "Straight to the sick tent," she reminded her.

"He closed it up when you left," Faith said.

They passed the first few tents on the road. No people came to greet or stall them.

"And no one opened it again?" They made it through the outer tents and Lena could see the large sealed one.

"You don't know how hard it is to act on anything when your belief in a leader is destroyed. And who would risk that you were wrong? That the sickness could be contagious. That it wasn't just poison."

I should have thought about that.

"How do you know your brother came? And the others?"

"He told me. I went in to talk to him and convince him to take the treatment. He said he was coming here and bringing anyone who could walk with him."

If only he'd made it, Lena thought. "But you didn't see anyone come?"

Lena looked at the tent. Someone had laced the flap closed. More tent pins than before held it tight.

"No. You think they've been locked in? It's a tent, not a prison."

Not for healthy people with something sharp to cut the

fabric. Lena pulled out her knife, ready to slice through the laces. "Is anyone else missing?"

"I don't know."

Faith was shaking in Lena's arm. "You stay here."

She helped Faith to sit beside the fire pit. Still, no one came to check what they were doing. The camp hadn't broken; the inhabitants were hiding somewhere, but Lena couldn't worry about that. They'd cracked Poorjohn's total control. Taking advantage of that had to be the next step. The sick people came first.

Lena ignored the laced flap. If she was right, it would be better to avoid official entrances. She slipped around the side and strode to the middle. Bending, she stabbed the point of her knife into the fabric close to the ground and sawed a hole big enough to step through.

The smell was like a living thing. Vomit and urine and feces and unwashed human. Light came from a few candles — stupid use of oxygen.

The noise came at her: moaning, crying, and rasped breathing.

Her choice of entry was right. Two men stood at the tent flap holding bats. The attendants from yesterday still walked the aisles, but they had nothing to offer but comforting words.

"Open this up," Lena commanded. "How can you do this to your people and still say you believe in God."

The two guards stepped toward her. She shifted to a fighting stance and adjusted her grip on the knife.

One of the guards moved into the aisle between two patients. A hand flashed out of the covers and pushed at the back of his knee. He buckled and the other patient jumped on his back to bring him down.

The second guard used more caution and swung at Lena with his bat, staying out of the range of her knife. Lena dodged but stepped backward. Fighting in the thick air and crowded floor was going to be impossible.

A metal pot flew through the air and hit the guard on his temple, the contents splashing over his face and clothes. He lost interest in the fight and tried to clean himself.

"Bring help." The words came from one of the attendants. "We can hold here for a while. You cannot free us alone."

Lena looked around her. The fight had made no sound. The two guards were bound and gagged. "You can leave if you can walk," she said. "Go to the farm."

"No," the same attendant said. "We will not leave the worst cases. And if anyone goes, it will signal Poorjohn. Go bring help."

It was the best option, but Lena's guilt at leaving them defenseless stopped her from moving. She looked at the slice in the fabric. Would it be better for them to close it, or would the fresh air be more valuable?

"It won't take long. I'll tell Faith to keep watch and warn you if anyone is coming."

The attendant nodded and then shoved her through the opening.

CHAPTER THIRTY-FOUR

Lena wasted no time running for the farm. She noticed Faith slip away as she passed the cluster of tents forming the outer boundaries of the camp.

"Grab guns," she shouted, running for the kitchen. "Where is everyone?"

"We're all here," Evan said. "We figured you'd need us."

She explained what Poorjohn had done to the sick. "I don't think it's safe to try to cure them in that tent. We need to send everyone here. We might find more than just poisoning to deal with."

Deb grabbed a stack of old towels. "I'll get ready. I need a couple of helpers; Maya and Mahir will be the best. That leaves you with all the adults on your team."

The kids followed Deb without comment, but Mahir smirked at his sister as if saying 'look how important I am. You can't take me away.'

"Did you get a glimpse of Brian?" Ava asked. "If he's doing what we agreed, we could ruin everything by marching in and taking over."

She echoed Lena's fears. "No. Apparently, he's been holed up with the elders. I don't care, we can't let Poorjohn ignore those sick people any longer," Lena said. She knew there could be repercussions to the farm and to anyone who aligned with them. She no longer knew how far Poorjohn would go to win. It didn't really matter because if everything went right, no one would be hurt. "We don't use the guns for anything other than emphasis."

Keith handed her a rifle. "No. If we are taking them, we need to be prepared to use them. Last resort, but these aren't decoration."

Decisions made under this much stress and emotion were never great. Lena worried that everyone's last resort was different. "These people are weak and unarmed."

"As far as you know." Mellow checked her weapon. "We need to be able to act."

Mellow surprised Lena. Usually, it was Tik who took the hard view. Mellow was kind and thoughtful. "If we shoot without provocation, we are the bad guys."

"And if we don't defend ourselves, we are dead," Ava said. "Someone should be in charge of the decision."

Not me.

"Keith," Pallavi said. "He should tell us."

"Good idea," Lena said. "Our job right now is to bring those sick people here — all of them — and with no additional patients for Deb because of gunshot wounds."

The rest of the group agreed and waited for Lena to give the order to start.

"Stick together until we can free them. Then Keith, Evan, and I will stay to protect your back. Everyone helps the sick."

"And Poorjohn?" Ava asked. "He's the real problem."

"We will confront him. I have no desire to create a jail here. He has to go. If he's still in hiding, we'll confront him after you are safely back here."

"His followers?" Evan asked.

"Most are already leaving. I figure the people still there won't leave without waiting for a sick relative to be ready to join them."

Not staying to support Poorjohn? Lena felt hope rise. If Poorjohn lost his base, maybe he would go quietly. Even if he still fought, one man was easy to deal with.

Poorjohn stood with all the elders and Brian lined up in front of the prison that used to be a sick tent. The remaining camp inhabitants were crowded together in two groups gathered on either side. Faith stood with the larger one. Did that mean those were the people prepared to leave? There was no way for Lena to ask without giving Poorjohn a way to divert the conversation. And this time, she would be in control of what happened.

"Open that tent," she said.

"Those people have committed crimes," Poorjohn said. He mumbled something that Lena couldn't make out.

Lena noticed two of the four elders inch closer to Brian, but couldn't divert her attention.

"They are sick, and you denied them access to care." She resisted the urge to raise her gun. All weapons were pointed to the ground as Keith instructed.

"Anyone wishing care could have come to you. We did nothing to stop them. You are simply resentful that they chose to trust in God."

Lena wanted to turn around and check to make sure her support was in place. If she trusted them, she wouldn't need to check, and if she wanted to look strong, she couldn't check.

"They are too sick to get out of a tent you laced shut and set guards on. I saw what was happening inside," she said.

Now she wished Faith had joined her to confirm with her own words.

"The true followers will not believe your lies," Poorjohn said. "They will remain pure and in God's grace."

"It is simple to show who the liar is," Lena said. "Open the tent. Let people see."

He was ready for that. Poorjohn might be a fanatic, but he wasn't stupid. He looked to the crowds. They had supported him in the past. Lena couldn't be sure they wouldn't fall under his spell again. "Belief does not require proof," he said, arms wide to encompass everyone in his world. "God told me this morning that we will overcome this assault by demons."

That gave Lena an opening. She looked to the larger crowd and found Faith. She spoke to the whole crowd but kept her attention on her ally. Was she really one? "Who here wishes to see the state of the tent and their loved one?"

Faith stepped out of the crowd.

"No," Poorjohn said. He hadn't anticipated her defection. His body tensed and his fists clenched.

"Let her speak," Brian said calmly. "You need her to speak before you prove she is not truthful."

Whether he intended it or not, Brian's words calmed the man.

"No. We need to do this in private. I will not allow my flock to be poisoned by the words of an unbeliever. In my tent." He pointed to Lena.

It might not be smart to go alone, but with him out of the way, the rest of her team could free the patients and find out who was still loyal to Poorjohn.

"Who else?" she asked.

"My trusted elders. Your husband."

Brian gave her a tiny nod. She wouldn't be alone.

"Fine. I need a word with my team."

Poorjohn gave a smile and waited. Perhaps he didn't

realize that when he focused his gaze over Lena's shoulder it turned the smile into something creepy.

"This is the opportunity," Lena said, her voice even. "Get the sick out of there and find out who is still willing to follow Poorjohn."

"Be careful," Keith said. "Don't give up your weapon."

"Brian will be there too," Lena said. "He won't let them hurt me."

"I'm not as sure of that as you," Keith said. "If you aren't back in an hour, we're coming in."

She hoped it wouldn't take that long. All she needed now was to move the camp along. The sick would be cured, and by the end of the week, the farm would be theirs again.

CHAPTER THIRTY-FIVE

Inside Poorjohn's tent, Lena regretted her assurances that her ex-husband would protect her. Brian stood with the elders. She was alone. Brian wouldn't hurt her, but she didn't know if he would stop anyone else from doing it.

Poorjohn paced, muttering. Now he that had no audience, he let go of his control.

The elders watched Poorjohn. Three men and a woman. The men were well fed and bigger than Lena; the woman sharp-eyed and tensed for action. Against one of these people, she would have a chance, but not against all. By the time she raised her weapon, it would be too late, and she wouldn't be the one to start the fight.

She stepped back toward the flap, unwilling to turn her back on anyone.

"I'm going back to my friends," she said. "Anything you want to say can be said out there."

"No." Poorjohn flicked his fingers at his elders. One of them moved to guard the door. "You will listen in here."

Lena looked at Brian. He looked away. "Okay, say your

piece and let me go. If you keep me in here, my friends will come, and they won't stop until I'm released."

"This world is not a good place," Poorjohn said. "You know that."

"It's as good as the people who live here," she said. Feeding his paranoia was a bad idea — denying it, probably just as bad, but Lena couldn't think what else to do.

"And the people who live here are good?" Poorjohn stalked toward her. "Have you not committed sins? Have you not killed?"

She didn't answer. He wasn't looking for a conversation.

"The first warning was the plague," Poorjohn continued. "When I lost my children and then my wife, I turned to the church and they were no help. They said there was a plan and we should keep our faith in the scientists."

He waited for her to give her opinion.

"I had no faith. For two years, I grieved at the bottom of a bottle, pills and alcohol. My family was my life. I could not find the strength to kill myself." He started pacing again. "I thought for a long time that I myself was too evil to live. Those years were a test. One night I ran out of poisons. Pain tortured me. The next night the pain lessened. By the third night, my mind became clear and that is when God spoke to me."

He sat and wiped sweat from his face. "Those people out there are my new family. I will not let them go."

He was calmer now. Lena couldn't be sure if it would last. She looked to Brian. The elders stood with him again. This time a little closer as if to signal a shift in alliance. If he had turned them into allies, and they were following his direction, she wasn't in danger from anyone but Poorjohn.

"I see you," Poorjohn said.

Lena turned her attention back to him; his words were addressed to the elders.

He pointed at Brian. "This man is false. God speaks to me."

No one spoke. No one moved.

"You wish to leave? I will not stop you." His voice was weary.

Lena took a step toward the tent doorway.

"Not you. My family will leave. You will stay. Your husband will go."

The elders slipped past her before Lena could say anything. Brian stopped beside her on his way out. She couldn't read his expression. Every movement was controlled. "Remember you have a gun." He waited until Lena nodded. "Try not to use it."

He left her standing in the tent without a single ally. She hoped he had a plan and it didn't need her to guess at her role. The least he could do was tell the others that Poorjohn finally lost his grip on sanity. But he was right. She had her gun.

Poorjohn sighed. "We are alone. Please sit and we can talk."

He sounded rational, but knowing it couldn't be real, Lena remained where she stood. "What do you want to say?"

"Why do you hate God?"

"I don't. I hate what you are doing. You came here and took my land. You blocked the road. You starved your people. You led them astray. You poisoned them." She took a breath. "And you say that is God's work."

"All tests. God tests us." He reached for a jug and a glass. "At least drink some water. You must be thirsty."

"I don't want to be poisoned."

He drank from the glass and smiled. "See? It's safe."

Lena didn't want to drink, but as soon as he mentioned thirst, she felt parched. But this wasn't a social event, so she shook her head. She wouldn't leave until she knew his plans, but every nerve in her body was telling her to run. She couldn't. This was the first opportunity she'd had to observe the man without the performance. Possibly the only opportunity to get to the truth. "What are you going to do now?"

"I will continue with my mission to save people." He stood and started pacing again. "People are in pain. I can help them."

As much as she wanted to solve the problem, this was beyond Lena's expertise. She knew that if his faith was real, no logic would penetrate. If something in his past caused the fervor, nothing she said would convince him to change his mind.

But is that true? We all know grief. If this is all stemming from the loss he experienced, I should be able to find common ground.

"Your pain will not heal others," she said. "We all lost people, but we survived. We need to live our lives in gratitude for that. Whoever or whatever made us the survivors of the plagues, we can't just throw the gift away."

"In the New Eden, there will be no pain." His pacing sped up, and he moved closer to her as he circled the tent.

Lena shifted the rifle in her hands to make it easier to raise fast. She could think of nothing else to say. There was no revelation here for Poorjohn. If he managed to heal, it would be a long and difficult journey. One he would undertake elsewhere.

He stopped pacing. "I can show you," he said, the gleam of fanaticism back in his eyes.

Lena's compassion faded. This man was dangerous no matter what caused him to act this way. She would be forced to offer him something she didn't want to so she could free herself. He needed to be restrained, but to do that, she had to escape. "I have no wish to die here," she said.

He rushed toward her.

Surprised, she raised the rifle.

Too late, he batted it away and grabbed her arm. The fanaticism in his eyes now brilliant.

This can't be happening.

It wasn't a simple power play. Poorjohn was going to hurt her. Lena punched at him, hoping it would break the madness, but he didn't let go.

She scratched his face, but he didn't flinch. Nothing seemed to penetrate the blaze of madness.

She opened her mouth to scream. He twisted her arm to make her turn her back to him. He pulled her close, and then his hand covered her mouth.

Lena waited for him to kill her. She should have been more careful. Brian's words had shifted her off guard. Poorjohn was too strong for her to break his grip. He held her too tight for her to twist out of his control, too close for her to disable him.

"What was that?" he whispered. "Did you hear it?"

Lena nodded, hoping he wouldn't ask her what she'd heard. Because the fighting had taken all her focus — or there had been nothing to hear.

He loosened his grip. Lena took the chance and pulled free.

Every muscle of her shoulder blazed with pain as she struggled until he let her go.

Now she heard something: shouting outside. The crowd was calling for Poorjohn to show himself. Anger hardening the sounds.

He stood staring at the tent flap, appearing lost in some fantasy. Lena picked up her rifle and nudged him back to the chair. Until she found out what the crowd wanted, she would keep him safe here. Whatever had tipped him from manic to catatonic could easily reverse. He had to be restrained. He gave no resistance when she used her belt to tie his arms. She tore his bedsheets to make rope and tied him to the chair.

When he was secure, she stopped to breathe. The pain in her body rushed in. She sat across from him, waiting for the wave to subside enough that she could face the problem outside.

CHAPTER THIRTY-SIX

A few minutes later, Lena stepped into the sunlight. Brian stood in front of Poorjohn's followers. He was saying something to them.

Twenty or thirty people crowded forward, yelling for Poorjohn. She looked around. There were fewer tents. People had left.

"What's going on?"

Brian turned to her. "Where is he?"

"Safe."

He turned back to the crowd. "We have him contained. No one will be exacting revenge today."

The crowd quieted but was still restless.

Faith walked toward them from the direction of the sick tent. "Everyone is gone for treatment. Why are these people gathered?"

"They want Poorjohn to pay," Brian said. "But I won't let them do anything rash. They are angry and will regret whatever they do. Can you calm them?"

"Can we feed them?" Faith asked. "They are starving. A meal will distract them."

Brian looked to Lena.

She stepped toward the crowd.

"A meal will be prepared. Is there someone who can help with that?"

For a moment, no one spoke. Then two people stepped forward.

"How do we know you aren't lying?" the man asked.

"The food will be appreciated. We will wait for judgment, but he must pay for what he did to us." The woman patted the man's arm.

"He is ill," Lena said. "Go help with the sick. I'll tell my family to feed you. We will talk about punishment later."

She turned away, not willing to answer the question about lying. "Brian, can you let Mellow know about the food. I think we can afford one good meal for these people. Something we can bring here. I don't want them crowding the patients. They will be leaving soon. No argument."

"We'll talk later. The elders are waiting for you." He pointed to the four people standing to the side of Poorjohn's tent.

Lena approached and said, "He is restrained, and I have no idea what to do with him."

The woman stepped forward. "I am Wisdom," she said. Then, with a little shake of her head, "No. That life is over. I am Teresa Garcia. Will you allow us to take him with us?"

These people had supported Poorjohn. When or even if they had stopped supporting him was unclear. She couldn't let them just take him away without knowing their plans. Now that the end of this nightmare was here, she found herself worried about what would happen to the missionaries. Death found people too easily on the road.

"Where will you go?"

One of the men stepped up beside Teresa. "I am Dae Pak, and this is Larry, and the other man is Kalvin."

If knowing their names was supposed to change her feelings about them, it didn't work. These people stood by while Poorjohn played his games and almost killed people.

"I asked a question."

"We will go from here," Kalvin said. "Why do you need more than that?"

"Kalvin, stop. She is not the enemy. She never was." Dae held up his hand to stop the man from saying more. "We will not harm him. He needs help."

"The people he harmed want justice," Lena said. "Why didn't you help him before? You could have saved everyone all the pain and deprivation he caused."

"We didn't know what he was doing. And is it justice they want?" Teresa asked. "You mean they want revenge. That will not help anyone. Let us take him away."

The crowd needed some satisfaction, or they might turn on the farm. She wouldn't allow them to kill Poorjohn, but neither could she just let him slip away.

"He's tied up in his tent. I think he's had a breakdown. I'd like Deb to look at him before we decide anything."

She told them to guard him until everyone finished eating.

Lena moved through the crowd gathered in the center of the camp, eating the meal Mellow had prepared for them. Maya and Mahir mingled with the diners, filling mugs and offering more food.

Faith was right. The food calmed people, and something made them trust a host. Or perhaps these people trusted strangers too easily and would follow anyone who gave them hope. She had no desire to replace Poorjohn.

She reached the center and called for the attention of the crowd. "There are things I need to say."

The small conversations stopped; the eating did not. Faces turned her way, expectant.

The only sound was Poorjohn ranting from his tent. No one seemed able to calm him, and he refused Deb's tea. He'd been in deep conversation with his demons, or perhaps God, since she left him.

"Some of you need medical attention. Please see our nurse after you've eaten. We will not turn anyone away. We want to give you help to start your journey."

Everyone stared at her. She hoped they were listening, not waiting for her to pronounce sentence on the man in the tent or offer them a paradise that no one was able to actually create.

"If you are not waiting for help, or for one of the sick to heal, I want you to prepare to leave. You must go soon to avoid winter on the road."

"Where will we go?" She couldn't identify the speaker but was grateful for the question. It showed one person was listening, at least.

"I suggest you head south to avoid the worst weather. There are settlements in that direction, bigger than here, but still small and in need of additional people. I'm sure you will find homes."

Brian joined her. "That is the best plan," he said. "It doesn't have to be permanent, but until next spring, you need homes. You have skills. You will be of use."

At least he was supporting her now, but she noticed he didn't close out the idea of them using their skills on the farm. And whatever the next problem turned out to be, maybe he wouldn't get in her way so much.

A noise behind her caught Lena's attention.

Poorjohn. He was free. Dae and Teresa stood beside him, each holding an arm, but not in restraint, in support.

What are they thinking?

"He was trying to hurt himself." Teresa pointed to Poorjohn's wrists, where a ring of welts blossomed blood.

Lena turned back to the crowd. A few people had risen to their feet, but no one came toward them. She'd almost won them over and now they were back on the precipice. They could as easily turn on her as on him. Either way, she had to stop any action that would lead to retribution.

She raised her voice so that all could hear. "We will tend his wounds. I will not allow you to take revenge. If you are able to travel, please leave before night falls. You will find places to rest along the road."

"They will not go," Poorjohn said, all madness gone from his voice. "They are faithful." Lena wondered if the craziness was faked and that Poorjohn was simply a con man. But a con man would know when to stop the grift.

Brian touched Lena's hand, making it clear whose side he'd joined, before he said, "Look around, reverend, most of your followers are gone."

"These are the chosen," Poorjohn said. "They are still here for a reason. They still believe in the new Eden."

Lena looked back to the people eating. Most of them could be waiting for the sick to be ready, but some might be still willing to follow Poorjohn. Was there something she could say to stop them? Was it her responsibility?

Then everyone who was standing turned their backs and headed toward tents. Five others stood and followed.

"I'm sorry," she said, turning back. This is what she wanted, but the feeling of sadness for this poor disillusioned man came as a surprise.

Poorjohn's face was drained of all color. His knees buckled and he sagged in the elders' grasp.

"Take him to Deb," she said. All they could do was bind his wounds. The damage inside his head was beyond the medications in Deb's box.

CHAPTER THIRTY-SEVEN

Half of the sick people were well enough to go. Deb wanted them to stay another day, but none agreed to. It was like they needed to get far away from the events of the last few days.

"If you really think it's a bad idea," Lena said to Deb, "we'll make them stay. But I think they want to move away from what happened."

"I can't make them," Deb said. "They all have families, or a friend, to help. I've advised them to take it slow, but frankly, with them gone, we can concentrate on the most critical cases."

None of them had offered to help care for their fellow missionaries. The community that had gathered appeared cohesive only a day ago. Now it seemed like everyone only cared for their own families. Lena felt the judgment in her thoughts. Perhaps they weren't selfish, just hurt. And maybe whatever pain made it possible for them to follow Poorjohn had healed by watching him deteriorate.

"How long for them? The worst cases."

"There are ten people left. Two of them will be fine in a couple of days. One of them... I don't know if she'll make it.

And she does not appear to have friends or family. The rest? They can hit the road by the end of the week."

"Maybe the elders will take the last one?" Lena didn't hold out much hope for them to show kindness.

"She's old and weak, anyway. I don't think it will be a problem if she needs to stay."

Lena heard the pain in Deb's voice. Hoping a patient will die is wrong. "Do your best. If no one will take her, she stays with us. The kids could use a grandma."

"May we speak?" Teresa and Dae stood looking up at her from the bottom of the porch stairs.

"Poorjohn?" Lena asked.

"Yes. We would like to take him with us," Dae said. "He is calm now."

"Deb, did you check him out?"

"Yes." She wiped her eyes. "I'm not trained in mental illness. His body is fine. He can travel. His mind... I don't know." She slipped past them and headed for the patch of shade covering her patients.

Lena wondered again if Poorjohn's condition was just an act.

"I wasn't planning to punish him," she said. "Most of the followers are already gone. It should be safe for you to take him."

"Thank you," Teresa said. "Are you aware of the reason we are his elders?"

Lena didn't care, but they seemed to need closure. "Why?"

"I was his sponsor in AA," Teresa said. "Before the plagues. Dae and Kalvin worked with him. Larry was his neighbor."

"So, you knew him. Why did you let him sink so far into the madness?"

"Because he was a good man before," Dae said. "Had

everything under control. Sober for ten years. Then he lost everything. I thought he would find his way through this. We couldn't have guessed he'd go so far. Everything he did was hidden from us."

Not the bullying and trying to take over the farm. But I don't need to solve this. They are going as far as I can send them.

"I don't think this is like an addiction," Lena said. "If you are sure he's not running a con, then he's mentally ill. This world doesn't have psychiatrists or drugs to help him."

"We are aware, but we won't abandon him," Teresa said. "Thank you for stopping it this time."

"Just take him away and don't let him gather a following again." Lena hoped they'd be successful but didn't want to know.

"Is Brian honestly planning to lead the flock?" Dae asked. "I guess they aren't a flock now. Our community?"

Lena held back her first response. Was that what Brian had been doing at the camp?

"You will need to ask him," she said.

Morning came before Lena found time to talk to Brian. She'd spent much of the night switching between relief he would be gone and anger he'd left her out of the planning. Relief won out. There was nothing she could do about his silence, and she would never need to deal with it again.

"Yes," he said when she asked him over tea.

Ava sat with them, but most of the others were tending the sick or checking the now almost empty camp. For the first time since he'd walked up the drive, they were virtually alone, and she had no urge to argue with him.

"They need someone to help them find a home," he added.

"But they've all split up," Ava said.

"No. I asked anyone who wanted to join me to wait a few miles from here. Don't worry, we will move on."

"I'm not sure you have the charisma to replace Poorjohn," Lena said. "Sorry, that sounded harsh. You know what I mean."

"I'm not offended. Those people appreciate my skills, and they need them. Someone needs to organize them. I won't let another Poorjohn, or someone like Newton Cole, take them. I won't make them worship anyone, and I won't stop them from worshiping unless they decide human sacrifice is a good choice." He laughed as though that wouldn't happen.

"Where will you go?" Lena asked. "As a group, they are too big for a community to take in. But you aren't that far behind the city refugees. Are you joining them?"

"South, like you said. Back toward New Surrey, I guess."

He would need supplies; they couldn't afford to give much. "There are some settlements within reach. When you came here, what did you pass?"

"I traveled mostly at night," Brian said. "It was safer, but I missed most of the sights."

"You're thinking of Millerville," Ava said. "It's been a while; not a good place. But maybe that's just my memories talking."

"What's there?" Brian asked, excited. "How far?"

Lena hoped Brian would make better memories there than she had. "It's a small town. Deserted as far as we know. Maybe someone has moved in by now. We ran into some trouble there, but that guy is dead, and he was the only resident left at the time. The houses were in good shape. Some of the stores remained, not much in them. You'll probably have to make war on vermin and insects to feel comfortable."

"How far?" Brian was hooked. "How long do you think it will take?"

It would be perfect, Lena thought. They could travel to

Millerville in a month or a little over. They'd find room for the whole community. There was land to farm close by. They would be able to expand. And they would be far enough away that visiting wouldn't be feasible.

"You'll be there before winter. We'll give you directions. Do you need anything for the trip?"

Brian smiled. "It seems everyone gets what they want this time. I'd like a few guns and some ammunition."

"We can do that." Lena would replenish the farm's supply when she delivered the produce they owed the alliance. She wondered if they could spare anyone to escort them. No. Too many people were gone already for her comfort.

CHAPTER THIRTY-EIGHT

A week later, the patch of land across the road was bare and ready for spring planting. No evidence remained that people had been there at all.

Lena reclaimed her peaceful spot on the porch with a glass of whiskey at the end of the day. Now was the time in the life of a farmer when things slowed down.

"It's nice out here," Keith said. Deb stood beside him, and they both held glasses of the latest effort at farm-brewed beer.

"Are you leaving soon?" Lena asked. It would be too late for them to set up if they didn't leave in the next week or two at most.

"We'll go tomorrow and check out the property," Keith said. "It will take a few days to winterize it."

"We'll come back," Deb said. "You're stuck with us until spring."

Relief settled on Lena. "You are welcome to stay forever."

"Did you talk to Pallavi?" Deb asked.

"Yes. Mahir wins. At least that's how he sees it," Lena chuckled at the memory of the victory dance the boy had done. "Evan and Pallavi are moving here. They'll travel to Prosperity tomorrow and be back in a week. Too bad his friends from camp all had parents. I mean, not too bad they weren't orphans, but he still has no friends his age here."

"You'll bring some here, I have no doubt. And, we have the winter to get everyone trained to replace us," Keith said.

"I hope the house will be full before winter," Lena said. "But yes. Mellow is going to push hard on you to create classes for her new school. I wish we could break ground now. It would be nice to have a bunch of kids around."

Spring would bring new life to more than the plants. The farm was changing, but for the good.

Deb patted Lena's shoulder. "We'll leave you to your solitude. It won't survive a pack of students."

Alone again, Lena sat back and closed her eyes, the sound of insects lulling her. A howl of a hunting wolf echoed from the hills. And then hooves.

Someone was coming.

Lena's rifle leaned against the railing an arm's reach away. When the same thing happened in the past, the sound had brought only problems. She put her glass down and prepared to shoot anyone bringing trouble.

"It's me," the rider shouted.

Jason.

Too soon. Someone had been hurt or killed. She went cold and then her mind took over the grief she was anticipating.

"Someone, come take this horse," Lena called into the house. "Jason, what's wrong?"

Mahir ran to take the reins from Jason and lead the horse to the barn.

"Nothing. Jeez, does there need to be something wrong?"

"You weren't gone long enough to settle those people anywhere. Is Scott hurt? Tik?"

The others crowded behind her. Ava ran past and hugged her son. Maya joined her. Jason couldn't reply until they released him.

"Everyone is good. Can I get a glass of water before I tell you?"

Water and a sandwich were gone before he spoke again.

"Thanks, I haven't eaten all day. I thought I'd be here sooner and didn't take enough supplies when we separated. Lesson learned."

"What happened?" Lena asked. Bad or good, she couldn't wait longer for the news.

"We didn't have to go too far to find a place. Scott and Tik got some of the city guys to scout as we moved. They found a town with only six people living there. A good place, they were welcome. We'd done our job."

"It took you a week to ride back?" Ava asked. "There's more, right?"

"Yeah. We stuck with the city guys until they got settled, a couple of days. And I guess I tried to talk Tik and Scott into letting me go with them for a few more days. No one was expecting me back for a while, right?"

Lena continued holding her breath, waiting to hear that someone had been hurt. Scott. He wasn't fully healed when he left.

"They wouldn't let me. Said my job was to come back and tell you the news."

"They were right," Ava said. "That's what we agreed."

"Yeah, and that is what they said."

"And?" Lena asked.

"Oh, yeah. So Tik says he misses you, Mellow. Scott said not to fall in love with Brian, Lena."

"Jason, what are you hiding?" Lena asked.

He threw up his hands in surrender. "There's a skill to storytelling. Okay, they will be back in a month. The plan is to go in a circle that ends here. They figure if they found a town no one knew about, we might find more places to scavenge closer than we thought."

No one died. They'd all be back together well before the first snow hit. There was no other shoe to drop. The realization didn't release the anxiety she felt. It would take a while for that to happen. Maybe when Scott was home, and she could touch him to make sure he was real.

"So, did anything happen here?" Jason asked.

WANT MORE?

Lena embarks on a journey across the continent to bring unity out of the chaos of the post-plague world. Use the QR code to get your copy of The Foundry and join the battle for the future.

If you enjoyed reading A Question of Sanctuary, please consider helping other readers to find the story by leaving a review.

WANT MORE?

———

FREE EBOOK

Claim your copy of A Choice to Make when you sign up for my newsletter and get a glimpse of Lena and Brian at the end of the plagues.

ALSO BY PA WILSON

For more books by P A Wilson

Use the QR code below or go to pawilson.ca

ABOUT THE AUTHOR

Perry Wilson is a Canadian author based in Vancouver, BC who has big ideas and an itch to tell stories. Having spent some time on university, a career, and life in general, she returned to writing in 2008 and hasn't looked back since (well, maybe a little, but only while parallel parking).

She is a member of the Vancouver Writers Social Group, The Royal City Literary Arts Society, and The Surrey Writing Workshop. Perry has self-published several novels. She writes the Madeline Journeys, a fantasy series about a high-powered lawyer who finds herself trapped in a magical world, the Quinn Larson Quests, which follows the adventures of a wizard named Quinn who must contend with volatile fae in the heart of Vancouver, and the Charity Deacon Investigations, a mystery thriller series about a private eye who tends to fall into serious trouble with her cases, and The Riverton Romances, a series based in a small town in Oregon, one of her favorite states. Her stand-alone novels are Breaking the Bonds, Closing the Circle, and The Dragon at The Edge of The Map.

For more information
www.pawilson.ca
pawilson@pawilson.ca

ACKNOWLEDGMENTS

People think that the process of writing is solitary. That's not the case for me. I have help from so many people it would be hard to acknowledge everyone, but I'll give it a try.

The support and inspiration I get from my writer's groups is incalculable. The Vancouver Writers Social Group opens my mind to other ways of telling a story. The Royal City Literary Arts Society gives me the opportunity to meet and share with other writers who have more knowledge than I do. The Other 11 Months group is where I learn about getting the words on the page. And my critique group who helps me find the best parts of the story I want to tell. Thanks to all of the members of these great groups.

Last of all, but definitely a huge part of the process, my beta readers. These are the people who love stories and are willing, and more than able, to tell me if my finished story is ready for you, my readers.